ANGEL
IN MY
BACKPACK

ANGEL
IN MY
BACKPACK

MARY LOU CARNEY

ZondervanPublishingHouse
Grand Rapids, Michigan

A Division of HarperCollinsPublishers

ANGEL IN MY BACKPACK

Published by the Zondervan Publishing House
1415 Lake Drive, S.E., Grand Rapids, Michigan 49506

Library of Congress Cataloging in Publication Data:

Carney, Mary Lou, 1949–
    Angel in my backpack.

    "Youth books."
    Summary: A collection of thirty daily devotions, in which a guardian angel named
Herbie goes with a young boy to summer camp to help him have a good time and
teach him about God.
    1. Youth—Prayer-books and devotions—English. [Prayer books and devotions]
I. Title.
BV4850.C35 1987   242'.2   87-14246
ISBN 0-310-28501-1

Illustrated by Mark Lindelius
Edited by Pamela Hartung and David Lambert

Printed in the United States of America

96 97 98 99 00 01 02 / DH / 15 14 13 12 11 10 9

for
Dick Marsh
and
all my friends at
CAMP TECUMSEH
(Brookston, Indiana)
where
"I AM THIRD"
is a way of life
and
the SON shines
all year long

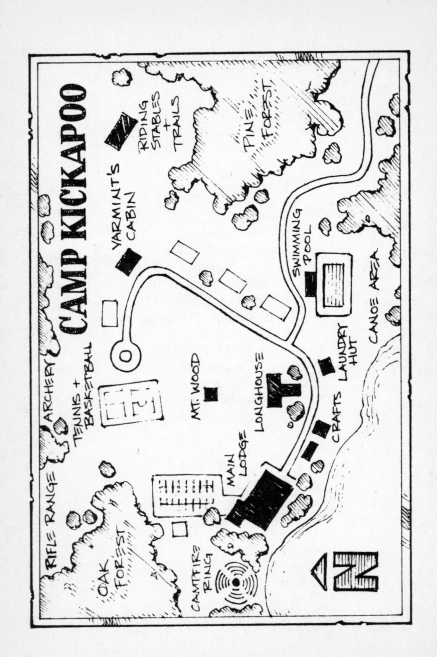

This is a book of daily devotions ...

It may not *look* like a devotional book, and it certainly doesn't *read* like one.

But it is.

We wanted to give you a different kind of devotional book. We thought you'd have more fun with it. And we thought you'd be interested in Mick, a junior-high kid just like you who happens to be spending his first summer at camp and who also has something most kids don't have— a pint-sized guardian angel named Herbie.

So choose a good time during the day to spend with God and read a chapter.

Thirty chapters.

Thirty days.

You don't have a Herbie in your life—at least not that you can see and talk to. We just made him up. But we hope Herbie and Mick—two made-up characters—will help you to think about a God who is real. And about how that God can make a difference in the everyday problems *you* face—at summer camp, at school, and at home.

Day 1

Mick grabbed the stalk of the weed and pulled. Hard. "Come on, you stupid weed!" he grunted. Suddenly the weed snapped a few inches above the ground, and Mick fell backwards. "Now I have to dig up the roots," Mick complained to an earthworm wiggling out of the widening hole. "I hate plants."

"But you certainly enjoy the hamburgers and french fries down at Bob's Burger Stop," said a voice. "And you couldn't have them without green grass for cows to eat and plump potatoes for cooks to peel."

Mick stopped weeding. He whirled around and looked in every direction. Nothing. He looked toward the garage. "Who's in there?" But the only sound was the tinkle of windchimes blowing in the breeze. Except there wasn't any breeze.

A hummingbird swooped onto a nearby flower. Mick kept pulling weeds—but he noticed that the humming continued even after the bird had flown away. In fact, it sounded as though whatever was humming was carrying a real tune. Suddenly he sat still and stared at the garden patch. Someone—or some*thing*—was humming "Row, Row, Row Your Boat"!

Mick clutched the spade. "Come on out! I got you covered!" The humming stopped and again the sound of windchimes tinkled across the yard.

"'Squashed by a shovel.' Now that would look tacky on my first day's report." And from behind a cabbage head appeared a tiny creature. He was dressed all in white, and huge silky wings fluttered on his back. He dangled a few inches above the ground, like a helium balloon.

"Aliens!" Mick yelled. "Oh, boy! I knew they'd pick me. Where's your ship? Do you have a laser gun?"

The creature flew up and sat on top of the cabbage. Then he straightened his halo and brushed a ladybug from his robe. "Get real, kid. Do I look like a monster from some science fiction flick?"

Mick looked at him. "No. As a matter of fact, you look a lot like one of the angel figures in our nativity scene."

"Bingo, kid! You've got it. That's exactly what I am. Herbekiah's the name; Herbie for short."

"I—I'm not going to die or anything, am I?"

"Hardly!" Herbie laughed. The sound of windchimes again. "You're leaving for camp in a couple of days and I'm going with you."

"Really?" Mick asked. He lay down on his stomach and looked Herbie in the eye. "Why?"

"Because you're scared. Because you don't really want to go. Because you *need* me."

"Hey," Mick said, sitting up and gesturing with the spade. "I can't wait to get to camp! It'll be the time of my life! I'm crazy about the idea! Just ask anybody."

"Aliens!" Mick yelled. "I knew they'd pick me!"

"I don't have to ask anybody, kid. I know how you *really* feel." Herbie pulled a tiny spiral notebook from his sleeve. "Camp," he said, flipping through the pages. "Ah, here it is. Camp Kickapoo: 'Hiking and swimming and sleeping out. Chapel and pillow fights and horseback riding.' Doesn't sound so bad."

"Oh, yeah," Mick said. "There's some things you haven't written in there."

"So tell me," Herbie said, producing a sharpened pencil.

"Well," Mick began as he sat cross-legged on the dirt, "there's camp food. They'll probably feed us bean sprouts and prunes and junk like that. The mosquitoes will eat me alive! And I won't know *anybody*. Everybody will probably think I'm weird or something. And I'm not exactly the world's greatest athlete." Mick sighed. "And I'll have to be away from home so long. What if I get homesick? What if the kids in my cabin hate me? And my counselor will probably be a cross between a Blue Beard and King Kong!" Mick jabbed the spade deep into the dirt.

Herbie flew over and sat on Mick's knee. "Cheer up, kid. I'll be with you the whole time you're at camp. Everywhere you go, I'll go. My job on this assignment is to make sure you have a good, safe time—and also to teach you a few things."

"Like how to go off the high board in diving?"

"Well, not exactly. But there are some other important things God wants you to learn at camp, too."

"Mick!" Mom called from the back door. "Dinner's almost ready."

"How about Mom?" Mick asked. "Can she hear and see you?"

"No way," Herbie said, spreading his wings and chasing a passing butterfly. "I'm *your* guardian angel. No one can see or hear me except you." Herbie disappeared around the house after the butterfly.

"Wow! My own guardian angel. It's even better than meeting an alien!"

"Of course it is," Herbie whispered into Mick's ear. Mick jumped and screamed. Herbie laughed his windchime laugh. It was then Mick noticed that Herbie's teeth were gold. All of them!

Mick picked up the spade and the pile of pulled weeds. "Think I'll really have a good time, Herbie?"

"Sure, kid," Herbie said. "You see, people aren't like plants—meant to take root in one spot and never have any new experiences. God gave them feet instead of roots so they could go to church and school, so they could shop and visit friends, so they could go to birthday parties and ice cream parlors—"

"And camp, right?"

"Right!" Herbie said, settling himself on Mick's shoulder. And the golden glint of Herbie's smile made Mick smile, too.

* * *

"See, I am sending an angel ahead of you to guard you along the way and to bring you to the place I have prepared. Pay attention to him and listen to what he says."

Exodus 23:20–21

Day 2

You ever been camping before, Herbie?" Mick asked as he laid his Bible in the top of his backpack.

"Let's see," Herbie said, scratching his head through the opening in his halo. "I spent a little time at Valley Forge with General Washington, but I don't guess you could really count that." Mick knelt in the middle of his bedroom floor, rolling up his sleeping bag. "And then there was that forty years in the wilderness."

Mick stopped tying the strings on his bag and stared at Herbie. "Forty years? Why so long?"

"It all started in ancient Egypt. The children of Israel were God's chosen people, and they had been forced into slavery by the evil Pharaohs and their brutal taskmasters. God heard their groaning and sent Moses to deliver them."

"I know this story. I saw it on the late, late show."

"You ought to read the book. It's even better than Technicolor. The story's found in Exodus, the second book of the Bible. It tells about the exodus, or exit, of all those hundreds of thousands of Israelites and all their flocks and herds from Egypt.

"After several days of some really tough hiking, they made camp beside the Red Sea. Meanwhile, Pharaoh, who was a really rotten guy, summoned six hundred chariots and an army of men on horseback. Soon the Israelites saw

Angel in My Backpack

huge clouds of dust on the horizon, and they knew they were in real trouble! They were trapped between Pharaoh's warriors and the Red Sea. They began to grumble and doubt God and wish they'd stayed in Egypt."

"So what happened then?"

"I thought you saw the movie."

"I did," Mick said. "But I think I fell asleep right about here."

"Well," Herbie said, "what happened was that God commanded Moses to hold out his rod over the water, and a wind began to stir. And then blow. And finally rage until it had rolled back the water of that great sea, leaving a path right through it. Then all the people—fathers, mothers, grandparents, aunts, uncles, cousins—marched through on dry ground. So did their sheep and goats. And when the very last Israelite had set foot on the opposite bank, guess who came thundering up to the water's edge?"

"Pharaoh—with his horses and soldiers."

"Right. They took one look at those huge walls of water and said, 'Anything those low-life Hebrews can do, we noble Egyptians can do better.' So they started across the pathway between the water. Their chariot wheels dug deep into the sand. The Israelites on the other side watched, wondering if they would all be killed when Pharaoh crossed the Red Sea."

"But he never made it across, did he?" Mick asked.

"Nope. God told Moses, 'Stretch out your hand.' So he did, and the wind softened to a whisper and then stopped completely. Suddenly the walls of water crashed around Pharoah. The horses stumbled and fell. The chariots overturned. And when at last the waters were quiet, not one Egyptian was left alive."

"Is that when the forty-year campout began?"

"You could say that. The Israelites were on their way to Canaan, a prosperous land God promised to give them. But it took them a long time of living in tents and roaming around in the desert before they trusted God enough to take possession of the land."

Mick tucked the sleeping bag under his arm and grabbed the suitcase with his other hand. He and Herbie started toward the garage. "And all that time—those forty years—God was with Moses and the people?"

"God is always with his people. Then *and* now," Herbie said. Mick put his suitcase in the back seat of the car and threw his sleeping bag in on top of it. "God still parts seas, kid. And not just seas of water. Sometimes they're seas of fear and homesickness, too. Moses didn't know what to expect out there; he didn't have a brochure or a map. But he did have God to guide him. And so do you."

Mick went back inside for the rest of his things.

Well, God, he prayed, *that was really something— what you did to Pharaoh and his warriors. I guess handling a few mosquitoes and a cabin of new kids at Camp Kickapoo won't be hard for you at all. So help me, God, like you did Moses and those other campers so long ago.*

Herbie settled into the top of Mick's backpack. "Let's go, kid. And don't worry so much. Things can't get too bad when you've got an angel in your backpack!"

* * *

"As I was with Moses, so I will be with you; I will never leave you nor forsake you."
Joshua 1:5

Day 3

 ick finished rolling out his sleeping bag on the top bunk and fluffed up his pillow. He looked at the bunk below his, covered with comic books and candy wrappers, and wondered—for the hundredth time—who would be sleeping there.

"Welcome to the mosquito capital of the world!" Mick looked up to see a red-haired boy about his own size standing at the foot of his bunk. "My name's Chris, but everybody just calls me Spike." He smiled, poking his fingers into his short, spiked hair.

"My name's Mick."

"This'll be my seventh summer," Spike said proudly. "Has Varmint been in here yet?"

"Varmint?"

"He's our counselor. That's what we call him because he can make so many animal sounds. Wait till you hear his horned owl—it's great!"

Mick followed Spike out onto the porch of the cabin. "Let's see what's happening over at Mt. Wood," Spike said, jumping over the railing and landing in the grass.

"Mt. Wood?" Mick asked as he came down the porch steps.

They headed toward a huge wooden structure sitting in the middle of the camp. "It's a wooden 'mountain' with slanted blocks of wood that let you really get the feel of rock climbing," Spike said. "It's really fun. You'll have to try it."

Mt. Wood didn't look like fun to Mick. When he leaned back and stared up its steep sides toward the tiny tower on top, he felt dizzy and his knees went weak.

"Hey, Spike! So you made it back again this year!"

"Flounder!"

Mick stepped aside as the two boys went into an elaborate routine of clapping hands and slapping legs, ending in a double handshake. Spike grabbed one of Flounder's bags. "I'll help you get settled."

"Let's hurry so I can claim a bottom bunk. I'll never make it onto a top one this year!" Flounder bounced his belly and laughed.

Together Spike and Flounder hurried toward the cabin on the far side of the field, and Mick stood alone in the shadow of Mt. Wood. All around the playing field little groups clustered together, laughing and talking. Mick crushed a dandelion that was growing near his foot.

"So, kid, how's it going?" Herbie floated down, like a snowflake on a still day.

"Terrible!" Mick muttered. "I hate it! Everyone knows everyone else. I feel like a cross between the invisible man and the boy with bubonic plague! I want to go home. Now!"

Mick realized that a group of boys had stopped and was staring at him. He felt his ears burn.

"You okay?" the biggest one asked. Mick nodded. "Wanna play some touch football?" Mick swallowed hard and shook his head. The guys ran on down the field, tossing the football.

"Why didn't you go with them?" Herbie asked.

"They didn't really want me to. They probably get extra privileges for being nice to weird kids who talk to themselves." Mick started back toward his cabin. "I'm going to take a nap. It'll probably be the most exciting thing I do all day!"

Later that afternoon, ten boys sat in a circle on the cabin floor. Varmint sat with them. "I'm your counselor, guys. For the next few weeks, I'll be your mother and your parole officer rolled into one." The boys laughed. "Here at Camp Kickapoo, our motto is 'I Am Third.' That means everything we do is done with this in mind: God is most important, the other fellow is second only to Him, and I am third."

A hollow *clung-clunk, clung-clunk* echoed across the playing fields as the bell rang for dinner.

"Time to eat!" Varmint said. "Wait until you taste those lobster livers we have every Sunday night!" Then he made a sound like a chattering squirrel.

The boys pushed their way out the door. "Who's the fresh fish?" one of them asked, pointing to Mick. The other boy shrugged his shoulders. Then both were gone.

Mick stood leaning against his bunk, the silkiness of his sleeping bag cool on his forehead.

"Time for dinner, kid," Herbie said softly.

"I hate it here, Herbie!" Mick buried his fist in his pillow. "I can't take a whole month of this!"

"You'll feel better after dinner."

"I'm not going to dinner," Mick said, walking outside. "Why bother?"

"Listen, kid," Herbie said. "To have a friend, you first have to *be* a friend."

Mick stepped off the porch and walked toward Mt. Wood. He sat down and leaned against its base. There was a soft sound—like someone crying. It came from a clump of trees nearby. Mick went to investigate.

Sitting in the grass was a little boy. Tears rolled from underneath his thick glasses. He looked up at Mick. "I wanna go home."

Mick sat down beside him. "Yeah, well, there's a lot of that going around."

"I don't know anybody. Everyone has a friend but me."

"I know what you mean," Mick mumbled.

"I hate it here! I hate it here!" He stared down at his shoelaces, fighting back more tears.

Mick was silent for a moment. "How about walking to the dining room with me?" he asked. "I don't want to go in by myself because, well—I'm a fresh fish."

The little boy looked at Mick for a long time. "Me, too," he whispered. "My name's Preston."

"Nice to meet you, Preston. And I'm Mick." Mick helped Preston straighten his shirt and finger-comb his hair. Then he smiled—and Preston smiled back. "Ready for dinner?"

"I think so," Preston said.

And together they walked toward the dining hall.

While Herbie, reclining on top of Mt. Wood, took out his spiral and beside **"LESSON 1: FRIENDSHIP"** placed a tiny gold star. "Good job, Mick. Now on to lesson two . . ."

* * *

If one falls down, his friend can help him up. But pity the man who falls and has no one to help him up!
Ecclesiastes 4:10

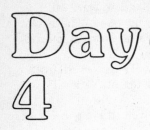

Day 4

Mick looked around for Spike and Flounder. The big veranda was filled with "Warriors"—boys and girls eleven to thirteen years old. The younger campers, the "Bucks," were already in their cabins, getting ready for bed.

"Over here, Mick!" Flounder yelled, waving his hand over his head.

"I hope you sprayed yourself with 'Eau de Camp,'" Spike said. Mick looked confused. "Bug spray! Those pesky critters munch us to death every night during Warrior Workshop."

A man with a guitar walked to the middle of the group and began strumming. "That's Buckeye," Spike whispered. "He's sort of our camp chaplain." Mick nodded. He remembered seeing Buckeye that morning during chapel.

The group grew quiet and together sang "Amazing Grace" while Buckeye positioned himself on a picnic table near the front of the porch. "Okay, everybody," Buckeye began, "let's divide into groups. Count off by five's." He pointed to a tall boy on his right, who sang out a squeaky "One!" The numbering continued until everyone had been assigned to a group.

Mick was a five.

Each group had a counselor for a leader and eight or

nine campers. Mick didn't know anyone in his group. The counselor introduced herself. "I'm Beaner. Tonight we're going to do a little 'ice breaker' to help us get better acquainted." She pulled a rolled-up sock from her sweatshirt pocket. It was taped several times with masking tape and made a soft sort-of ball. "Let's introduce ourselves. We'll start with you." Mick realized she was looking at him.

"Mick." He felt his throat tighten. "My name is Mick."

They went around the circle as other kids told their names. Gene, Beth, Christina, Critter, Julie, K.C., Stacey. Then each one took turns trying to name all the others. Mick was halfway around when he forgot the name of the tanned girl sitting opposite him. She smiled at his embarrassment.

"K.C. Her name's K.C." Mick looked up to see Herbie fluttering over K.C.'s head.

"K.C.," Mick said. And with renewed confidence, he managed to make it around the circle without a mistake.

Then Beaner took the sock-ball and said, "Now, I'll throw this to you and call your name as I do. Then you must toss it to someone else and call their name, too. Critter!"

Beaner tossed the sock to Critter, who caught it in his left hand. "Stacey," he said, passing it lightly to his right.

"K.C.," Stacey said, laughing and throwing it overhand. K.C. almost fell over backwards to retrieve it.

"Mick," K.C. called, smiling and tossing a perfect speed ball across the circle.

"Nice catch," Herbie said, sitting on Mick's tennis shoe. "And the way you handled the ball was pretty smooth, too."

"God has called you by name, Mick. He has chosen you ..."

"And now for our grand finale," Buckeye said. "Add a pair of shoes to the sock, and we'll have *three* things being tossed at the same time. Better call those names out loud and clear!"

Beaner contributed her battered Nikes, and soon Mick's group—like all the others—was convulsed in a session of naming and throwing and laughing.

Later that night, Mick lay on his top bunk listening to the even breathing and raspy snoring of his cabin mates. A glimmery light drifted toward him from the bathroom. Herbie landed lightly on the bottom rail of the bed. "Been brushing your teeth again, Herbie?" Mick asked.

Herbie nodded. "It isn't easy keeping the shine on these gold babies," he said, sliding a tiny toothbrush up his sleeve. "You did a good job remembering those names tonight, kid."

"Well, I had a little help." Mick smiled.

"How did you feel when someone called your name and tossed you that makeshift ball?" Herbie asked.

Mick thought for a moment. "Good. Important. Happy."

Herbie flew up next to Mick on the sleeping bag. "Nothing makes a person feel better than being called by name, than knowing he is recognized. Remember when you were in elementary school and being called-out for those recess kickball games was so important?"

Mick nodded his head, recalling the knot in his stomach whenever he thought he might be the last one chosen.

"Calling someone by name—or by a friendly nickname—is a special way of telling him that you know who he is, that you care enough to go to the trouble of using his name." Herbie paused. "It's that way with God, too, kid."

"What do you mean?" Mick asked, yawning and stretching out on his bunk.

"Well, God knows each one of his children by name. He doesn't just lump them into categories based on age or sex, on the color of their eyes or the size of their shoes." Mick felt a twinge and opened his eyes to see Herbie pulling on his big toe. "God has called you by name, Mick. He has chosen *you* to be on his team. The Creator of the universe knows who you are—and wants you to be part of his family."

"Wow," Mick yawned. "That really is an awesome thought. God has chosen me . . ."

But before Mick could finish the sentence, his head sank deeper into the pillow, and he was fast asleep.

"Yeah, kid," Herbie said, shooing a mosquito off Mick's pillow. "Awesome."

Wrapped in the soft sounds of night, all Camp Kickapoo settled into a sound sleep. And curling up in the top of Mick's backpack, Herbie did, too.

* * *

"I summon you by name . . . I am the Lord, and there is no other; apart from me there is no God."

Isaiah 45:4—5

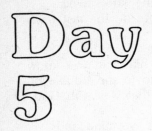

Day 5

"Guess you've figured out why they call you 'hopper' when you do dining room duty," Herbie said, as Mick set his heavy load of china plates on the table and hustled back toward the kitchen, dodging other hoppers.

"You bet I know why!" Mick huffed. "It's because we all hop around in here like spastic grasshoppers!" Jogging back toward his table with boxes of Cheerios and Raisin Bran, he almost ran into K.C., who was carrying a big pan of soapy water to the side counter.

"Sorry!"

"That's all right," K.C. said. "What this place really needs is a traffic control!"

"Yeah, and hired help instead of slave labor. Are you a hopper today, too?"

"Well, actually I'm more like a Super Hopper. I'm a Ranger. We do all the dishes, feed the scraps to Boris— the resident hog—and generally do whatever needs to be done around camp."

The tromp of feet told Mick the campers were filing in for breakfast. "Speaking of feeding hogs . . ." Mick said.

The boys in Mick's cabin sat at the big, round table. "Hey," Paul said, deliberately dropping his spoon on the floor. "My spoon fell. Get me another one."

Mick went to the kitchen and grabbed a handful of spoons. "Here," he said, shoving two into Paul's cereal.

"So where's the milk?" Spike asked. Everyone looked at Mick.

"I'll get it! I'll get it!" he said, scraping his chair on the wooden floor.

Mick was coming back to the table with a jug of milk in one hand and a huge platter of scrambled eggs in the other. Just as he passed the table where Critter's cabin was sitting, a boy wearing star-shaped sunglasses pushed back his chair. Mick tripped over the back chair legs and fell flat. The milk jug bounced against the floor. Scrambled eggs flew up in the air and landed everywhere, including Mick's hair.

"*Hey*—watch where you're going, clumsy," the boy with star-shaped glasses said.

"It wasn't my fault!" Mick yelled. The dining hall filled with laughter and yells of "clumsy" and "egghead." Mick looked down at the floor as he scooped up lumps of egg and threw them back on the plate.

"Hurry up with that milk," Spike yelled.

"And go get us some more eggs before they're all gone!" Paul demanded.

Mick slammed the jug of milk down on the table and stomped off for a new platter of eggs.

Finally, breakfast was over. Mick stood over the stack

Angel in My Backpack

of dirty plates and bowls, scraping scraps onto the empty platter. He looked up to see K.C. mopping the floor.

"So, how do you like the food business?" she asked, smiling.

Mick slid a slimy piece of jellied toast onto the plate of leftovers. "I hate being a hopper. Instead of coming back from camp with a suntan, I'll probably come back with dishpan hands!"

K.C. leaned on her mop handle and looked at Mick. "And what's wrong with dishpan hands?"

Mick waved the spatula in the air. "I've got better things to do with my time than wait tables and fix pig food!"

"Too good for this kind of work, huh?" K.C. said as she mopped the floor with long, firm swipes. "I'd better go now, back to the kitchen with the rest of the scumballs."

"K.C.!" Mick called, but she had turned her back to him and pretended not to hear. Picking up his stack of dirty dishes, Mick walked toward the kitchen.

"Well, if it isn't my favorite hopper," Herbie said. "How was breakfast?"

"How would I know?" Mick asked, sliding the plates through the window of the dishwashing room with a shove. "I spent the whole meal jumping up to get milk and eggs and butter and juice. I wish I'd never come to this crummy camp."

He went back to his table and began stacking the chairs on top of each other, making as much noise as he could.

"You know, kid," Herbie yelled above the din, "being a hopper is an important job."

Mick finished stacking the chairs and carried the boxes of cereal back to their shelves. "Why? Because it teaches me important things like how to fold napkins and scrape eggs off the floor?"

"No," Herbie said, "because it gives you the chance to be a servant."

"Oh, great. What's so special about that?"

"Well, for one thing, you're in good company. Jesus, too, was a servant."

"I thought he was a carpenter."

"That was the trade Joseph taught him, but Christ came to earth specifically to be a servant. He laid aside his majesty and power and pomp to become a man, to serve and help and work for the common people. And once, while they were all eating together, Jesus even washed the disciples' feet."

"You're kidding! Why?"

"To set an example. Jesus wanted to show his followers that there's no room in Christianity for self-importance, for thinking you're better than someone else."

"Sort of like Varmint's I AM THIRD speech?" Mick asked. Mick started toward the door. Out of the kitchen came K.C., carrying a big bucket of scraps.

"Need some help?" he called.

"Oh, no! Not from His Majesty Mick," she said.

Mick walked over to her. "Here, let me feed the hog. I really want to—as long as I don't have to wash his feet, too."

"What?" K.C. asked.

"Nothing," Mick laughed as he put his hand on the wire handle of the bucket. "Just let me do it, okay?"

"Why do you suddenly want to drag this pig slop down to Boris?"

"Because," Mick said, taking the bucket from her and walking toward the pig pen, "it gives me a chance to do something important."

* * *

Do not think of yourself more highly than you ought, but rather think of yourself with sober judgment, in accordance with the measure of faith God has given you.

Romans 12:3

Day 6

The pitcher stood still as a statue, except for the moving of his jaws as he chomped his bubble gum. Then he whizzed a fast ball over home plate.

"Strike one!" the umpire called.

"He's going to make an out. I can just feel it!" Jeff grumbled to Mick.

The pitcher straightened his star-shaped sunglasses, then tossed a curve ball. Spike whacked it and ran, sliding into first base.

"Safe!"

"Who's that pitcher?" Mick asked.

"Iceman," Jeff said. "That's what we all call him because he thinks he's so-o-o cool."

"Mick!" Varmint yelled. "Your turn at bat."

Mick walked to the plate, taking a few practice swings on the way. He faced the pitcher.

Iceman went into his windup, then stopped. A crooked smile filled his face. "Well, if it isn't egghead!" he said. "I might as well let you hit—you'll probably fall over your own feet before you make it to first base anyway!"

Mick clenched his jaw and swung the bat hard. "Just pitch the ball."

Iceman burned one across the plate. Mick swung—and nicked it with the end of the bat. It popped up high over

Angel in My Backpack

the pitcher's mound. "Got it!" Iceman yelled. Mick tore out for first, but he was only halfway there when he heard his fly ball land with a thick thud in Iceman's glove.

"Out!"

Mick trotted behind the backstop. "Tough break," Varmint said.

"Eggheads are used to tough breaks," Iceman yelled. "Eggs, break—get it?" Everyone in the outfield laughed. "Looks like the yolk's on you, egghead!"

Mick stomped into the dugout and over to the drinking fountain. He let the water run across his hot cheeks.

"What a jerk," Herbie said, sitting in midair and juggling stray drops.

"Who, me?" Mick asked, spitting out a mouthful of water.

"No! Iceman. He's one of those poor schmuckos who tries to make himself look bigger by making everybody else look smaller."

"Well, he did a great job out there. I wish he'd lay off."

That night, after lights out, Mick lay on his bunk. As he stretched out and closed his eyes, a buzzing hummed near his ear. "Stupid mosquitoes!" he grumbled, brushing the air with his hand.

"Not quite, kid."

Mick opened one eye. Herbie stood next to him on the pillow, hands on his hips. "Go to sleep, Herbie."

"I will. As soon as you finish saying your prayers."

Mick rolled over on his stomach. "I *did* finish them. I prayed for all the usual people—Mom, Dad, my grandparents. I even remembered to thank God for the hamburgers we had for dinner. What else do I have to pray about?"

"Iceman."

"Iceman? You've got to be kidding! Why would I pray for him?"

"Listen, kid," Herbie said, settling on the pillow next to Mick. "Prayer is not just a list of 'God bless' and 'thank-you's.' It's not just rattling off memorized lines. Prayer is communication. It's a time when you not only praise God, but you talk to God about your problems, too."

"And Iceman is *definitely* one of my problems!"

"The Bible is filled with answered prayers. Like Peter's chains falling off his arms when he was in prison in Acts 12. Or the widow's son being brought back to life by Elijah's prayer in 1 Kings 17. And what prayer did to Sennacherib in Isaiah 37 is incredible! And all these things happened because people brought their problems to God."

"But . . . I'm not sure how to pray about my problems. Do I ask God to get rid of them or what?"

"Just tell him how you feel, kid—what's bothering you, what you're afraid of, what makes you mad."

"Like Iceman?"

Herbie nodded.

Night sounds surrounded the cabin. Mick could hear Spike's bed springs squeak as he shifted in his sleep. Folding his hands, Mick began, *It's me, God. Mick. Herbie says you've been waiting to hear from me. So here I am. And I might as well start off with this guy who's been bugging me. His name's Iceman . . .*

Softly Herbie flew to the window. He hovered there in the moonlight, watching fireflies flit across the playing field. "We haven't heard the last of Iceman, kid," Herbie sighed. "I'd bet my halo on it!"

* * *

Do not be anxious about anything, but in everything, by prayer and petition, with thanksgiving, present your requests to God.

Philippians 4:6

Angel in My Backpack

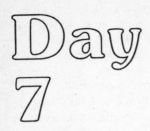

Day 7

"Wear scummy clothes!"
Spike laughed. "Today you're going to get dirtier than you
ever have in your whole life!"

Mick pulled on his old gym shorts and faded soccer
shirt. Herbie sat on the foot of his bunk watching. "Blah,"
Herbie said, grimacing. "Just talking about it makes my
mouth feel gritty!" Herbie pulled out his gold toothbrush
and flew toward the bathroom.

"Let's go, guys!" Varmint yelled.

Mick's cabin started toward the trails that led to Ghost
Creek. Soon they left the path to wade through inlets and
climb ravines until they came to a cove of shallow water.
The banks were gray and slick, like seal skin. The smell of
mud and stagnant water filled the air. High overhead a
crow cawed.

"Oh, mud! Beautiful, beautiful mud!" Spike scooped
up a handful and plopped it on his head. "How I've missed
you!" He knelt in the water and began covering his arms
with the gooey mud of the creek bottom.

"Let's try the slide!" Paul yelled. Half the boys
scrambled up on the bank and began pushing each other
down its incline. They landed with a "splash" and a
"thunk" in the green water.

"Look at me! I'm an alien!" Jeff piled mud high on
his head and stuck sticks like antennae on top of it.

Mick packed the foul-smelling mud on his chest and cheeks. Then he growled, "I'm King Kong!"

Soon everyone was covered with mud. Round, white eyes looked out of gray cocoons. Mick spotted Herbie reclining high above the mud hole on a birch tree limb. Mick smiled: Herbie held his nose.

As they reached the edge of the clearing, all the boys began to yell, "Mud hike, mud hike. Ooh-aah! Mud hike, mud hike. Ooh-aah!" The Warrior girls, who were playing tennis, squealed and ran.

The boys then made their way down to the river for the first of several washings. Mick leaned on the trunk of a willow tree, waiting for his turn. He watched the boys wade into the murky river, dip under, and rub at the clay-like coating on their limbs and clothes.

"This river is almost as muddy as you are," Herbie said as he fluttered a few feet in front of Mick, then settled himself on a big rock with feathery fern growing beneath it. "You know, kid, this reminds me of a Bible story."

"About one of your forty-year campers?"

"No. Naaman was a great commander in the Syrian army. He was brave and smart and well liked by the king. But he had one serious problem—leprosy."

"Wow, that is serious," Mick said. "I saw pictures in

Angel in My Backpack

National Geographic of some people in Africa who had
leprosy. It was gross!"

"It's also painful—and sometimes fatal," Herbie said.
"But Naaman's servant girl told him to go see Elisha,
God's prophet, and he would heal him. So Naaman started
off, loaded down with fancy presents for Elisha. He was
ready to perform any valiant deed the prophet demanded,
to pay whatever ransom was necessary. But instead Elisha
sent Naaman a message. He told him that in order to be
cured of leprosy, he must wash himself in the Jordan River
seven times."

"Sounds simple enough," Mick said.

"A little *too* simple for Naaman. The Jordan River was just about as dirty as this one will be after you all get through. Naaman was a proud man. The idea of dipping himself seven times in such mucky water disgusted him."

"So what'd he do?"

"Well, his servants finally persuaded him to try it. And when he came out of the water, his skin was as healthy and pink as a newborn baby's."

"Bet then he was glad that he'd gone for a dip in that ugly Jordan," Mick said, picking dried mud off his elbows.

"You better believe it!" Herbie flew closer. "Sometimes, kid, people begin to think they're 'too good' to do some kinds of work, too important to be seen with certain people, too big-time to be bothered with the common things of life."

"You mean they get 'stuck up'?" Mick asked.

"Uh-huh. They forget that in the eyes of God, everyone is the same. Whether their shirts have stains or preppy alligators on them; whether their eyes are slanted or round; whether their skin is pale as a full moon or dark as a starless night."

"Your turn, Mick!" Spike called from the bank of the river.

Mick stood up and started toward the water. "Hey, Herbie," he said. "Did you hear? Tomorrow we're going on another mud hike!"

"Wonderful," Herbie groaned. "There's nothing like good, clean fun!"

* * *

Live in harmony with one another. Do not be proud, but be willing to associate with people of low position. Do not be conceited.

Romans 12:16

Day 8

"Just remember," Beaner said, strapping on Mick's hard yellow helmet, "we've got you. You can't fall. Just do your best."

Mick looked up at Mt. Wood. It was so tall! Shafts of sun splintered through the openings on its roofed top.

"Good luck, Mick!" Flounder waved down from the tower. "And don't worry about a thing! Me and Spike've got you!"

Spike held the harness as Mick stepped into it. He snapped on the thick yellow rope that Flounder had attached to the pulley up above. "Go for it, Mick. You can do it!" Spike said, slapping him on the back.

Mick placed his foot on the first block and reached above his head for handholds. "A little to the left," Beaner said.

Mick moved his hand in that direction. He felt the short firmness of wood under his right foot as he pushed up and grabbed for a block. The slant of the wood dug into his palm. He found a block for his other foot and began his climb.

"Remember," Beaner yelled, "you've got four points of contact. Move one at a time. Push with your legs. Don't try to pull with your arms."

Mick could feel the sweat creeping down his back. Grunting, he slid his foot up to the next block. Then his hand. Other foot.

36   *Day 8*

"Come on, Mick!" Jeff yelled.

Mick's arms began to ache, as if he were trying to haul two tons up Mt. Wood. He reached up and felt his foot slip. He slid a few inches down the side of Mt. Wood, but the rope held him steady.

"It's okay," Beaner said calmly. "We've got you. To your right. Lift your foot to your right. Take deep breaths. Now, push up and reach again."

Mick fought back the panic that knotted his chest. And he climbed.

Mick fought the panic that knotted his chest ...

"All right, Mick ol' boy! You're over halfway now!" Flounder cheered.

Mick's fingers ached from gripping the edges of the wooden blocks. His calves throbbed.

"You can do it!" Varmint yelled. Mick's cabin mates took up the cheer.

Mick pressed his face against the side of the wooden structure and tried to breathe evenly. Sweat stung the corners of his eyes. His arms began to shake, and his

Angel in My Backpack

fingers lost their grip. He felt his handholds slip. But Spike held the rope tight, and Mick hung suspended where he had stopped climbing.

"You're okay," Beaner assured him.

"Don't quit now!" Spike yelled.

"I want down," Mick said breathlessly.

"You're almost there!" Varmint said.

"I want down!" Mick screamed.

"Let him down," Beaner said to Spike. "All right, Mick. Get back on the wall. Big step down to your left. Easy. It's okay."

Mick touched the ground and leaned against Mt. Wood while Spike and Beaner undid his harness and hard hat.

"You did well for your first try," Beaner said. "Want to try again tomorrow?"

"No," Mick said, turning to head for his cabin.

"Hey, Mick," Flounder called down. "Don't leave yet. Spike's gonna try to do the Mt. Everest climb."

But Mick was running by that time.

Mick stood in the shower, letting the water rush over him, feeling the tingle of tense muscles relaxing. Then he slipped on a pair of running shorts and stood looking at himself in the mirror. "Loser," he mumbled as he began to comb his wet hair.

"A little hard on yourself, aren't you?" Herbie asked, appearing on the ledge of the mirror.

"So where were you when I needed you?"

"Closer than you think," Herbie said. "Besides, you had Spike and Flounder and Beaner."

"And I still failed!" Mick threw his comb across the room. It landed with a crack against the cement blocks.

"Don't take it so hard, kid. Lots of people don't make it to the top of Mt. Wood their first try. Flounder didn't. Jeff didn't. Even Varmint didn't."

"Really?"

"Really. That's why they were cheering you on, encouraging you. They knew how it felt. They'd been there."

"It did help, having all the guys pulling for me like that," Mick said, picking up his comb and walking toward his bunk.

"It's that way with being a Christian, too, kid." Herbie took a quick look in the mirror at his gold teeth before he followed Mick. "Chapters 11 and 12 in Hebrews talk about the 'great cloud of witnesses' watching and encouraging from heaven—people like Abraham and Moses and Samson. They're up there urging you to keep climbing."

"Wow, a heavenly cheering section!"

"So sometimes, when you feel like you can't keep on, when you want to give up even trying to be a Christian, look up. And if you *really* listen with your heart, you'll hear them say, 'Come on, Mick. You can make it!'"

Mick pulled on a T-shirt and started for the door.

"So where are we off to in such a hurry?" Herbie asked, fluttering his wings to catch up with Mick.

"Back to Mt. Wood. Spike or Jeff or *someone* might need a little encouraging."

"Right, kid. And you're just the one to give it to them!"

* * *

May the God who gives endurance and encouragement give you a spirit of unity among yourselves as you follow Christ Jesus.

Romans 15:5

Day 9

And this," said Cubbie, walking out of the barn with a big brown sorrel, "is a horse. Basic model. No power steering or stereo. Four legs, two ears, and a built-in fly swatter." As if on cue, the horse swished her tail and sent several big horse flies scurrying. Cubbie led the horse to the hitching rail where eight others were already tied up.

Mick sat on the fence watching and listening. He had never before been this close to a horse. "Quite a beast, huh, kid?" Herbie asked, patting the neck of the horse closest to Mick.

"Think any of them will buck, Herbie?"

"Not these. Trail horses are a calm bunch. Not like those fiery steeds Pharaoh used for his chariots."

Cubbie adjusted the last saddle and clapped his hands. "Your attention, please!" All the boys looked at Cubbie. He began wiggling his ears and nose at the same time. He stuck out his tongue and crossed his eyes. The boys convulsed into laughter. "Now that," said Cubbie, "is what *not* to do while you're on your horse. It won't bother him, but it'll drive the squirrels along the trail nutty." Cubbie walked over to the line of horses. "Let me introduce you to your mounts," he said. "This is Tarquin, Lady, Copper, Arie, Blue, Dolly, James, IBM, and Murdock."

Cubbie touched each velvety nose as he spoke. The

horses stood twitching and swishing their tails at the stubborn flies.

"Which horse you want?" Spike asked Mick.

"I think I'd like to ride Dolly." Dolly was soft-eyed, with a broad, friendly back. She was the color of a vanilla milkshake and had a silver-gray nose.

"Okay, gentlemen," Cubbie said, bowing from the waist, "start your engines."

The boys scrambled off the fence and to the horses. Mick managed to get Dolly.

"Mount from the left. Stay away from their back legs. Hold the reins in one hand." Cubbie went down the line, helping kids up into the saddle. "This way, mate," Cubbie said in a perfect English accent. "Pull up with this little do-dad here on the saddle. I think it's called a horn, although I don't know why. I can never get it to make a sound."

Mick put his foot in the stirrup, pulled himself up, and threw his leg over. Dolly moved a little under his weight. Then she lowered her head to crop a bit of grass growing nearby.

Cubbie untied the horses and, leading the first one, walked down the trail ahead of the procession. "Wagons, ho! Watch out for wild Indians and mean chipmunks." The other horses followed. Mick and Dolly were last.

Angel in My Backpack

The trail led through a pine forest. Row on endless row of trees flanked the sides. Wild bushes crowded the path, and green twigs were pushed aside by horses' noses and riders' legs.

"Notice how the trees all grow in straight lines?" Spike asked over his shoulder.

"Yeah," Mick said.

"Wagons, ho! Watch out for wild Indians and mean chipmunks."

"That's because this used to be a Christmas tree forest. Someone planted them years and years ago and never came back to cut them. Pretty neat, huh?"

Mick looked at the trees. Their fluffy tops towered overhead. Shafts of sun slanted through the boughs. The only sounds were the squeak of leather saddles and the thud of hooves on crushed pine needles.

"Quite a place," Herbie said softly, settling himself on Dolly's head and scratching behind her ear.

"It's so peaceful," Mick said. "And so big. How old do you suppose these trees are, Herbie?"

"Thirty-five years, come next Thursday. I remember when they were planted. Just tiny seedlings. A thousand of them all in rows. Looked pretty puny at the time, but sun and rain and patience turned those scraggly starts into a real forest."

Mick looked up into the green canopy of tree limbs. "Looks like they reach all the way to the clouds. It's hard to imagine them tiny."

"Patience," Herbie said. "That's the key to their growth, their success. These pines stretched their arms to the sun and *slowly* became great."

"We're not just talking about trees, are we, Herbie?"

"Smart kid," Herbie whispered to Dolly. "Most great things," Herbie said, flying over to sit on Mick's shoulder, "begin small and grow. Plants, people. Even ideas and dreams. So learn a lesson from the pines, kid. Grow straight and tall. Dream big. But be willing to work and wait, too. All worthwhile things take time."

Dolly rounded a bend and Mick saw the stables. The horses walked up to the hitching rail and stopped. "Bye, Dolly," Mick said as he dismounted. "Thanks for the ride." He stroked her nose, and she replied with a soft whinny.

Cubbie took the reins. "Another victim escapes from the killer pines!" he said, making a scary face at a group of girl riders sitting on the fence. They giggled as Cubbie went into his vampire routine.

Mick took one last look at the pine forest. "Thirty-five years," he said quietly. "Wonder what I'll be in thirty-five years?"

"Old!" Herbie laughed.

While overhead the air was filled with the swoosh of wind, dancing in the Christmas-tree forest.

*   *   *

The end of a matter is better than its beginning, and patience is better than pride.

Ecclesiastes 7:8

Day 10

Spike finished lacing his high-tops and grabbed his tennis racket. "Gotta go, guys. If I'm late for my lesson, Dave'll make me spend the whole hour chasing other people's balls!" He ran out the door, swiping at imaginary serves.

"I better go, too," Jeff said. "I've got canoeing, and today is when we swamp them. If I'm not back by dinner, call the Coast Guard."

"I'm in archery," Mick said, rolling off his bunk. "Maybe today I'll hit the target instead of the straw!"

Soon Mick sat under a poplar tree, waiting for his turn to shoot. Audi, the instructor, was giving commands. "Straddle the line. Pick up the bow. Nock one arrow. Fire all arrows." The air was filled with the *brrung-g-g-thunk* of arrows whizzing through the air to their marks. When everyone had fired his arrows Audi yelled, "Retrieve all arrows."

"Ah, so this is archery," Herbie said as he floated down in front of Mick. "It took me a while to recognize it with those *plastic* feathers on the arrows. Things certainly have changed!"

"Some things never change," Mick said, picking at the bark on the tree trunk.

"What's wrong, kid?"

"I don't know, Herbie. I'm just tired of people always

44   *Day 10*

pushing me! 'Make your bed! Pick up those gum wrappers! Pay attention! Don't slouch! You can do it! You're not trying! I'm disappointed in you! What kind of attitude is that!' Know what word I hate most, Herbie? *Potential.* The very next person who tells me I'm not living up to my potential, I'm going to break his jaw! I thought things would be different here at camp—but it's almost as bad as being at home. There Mom expects me to be the best behaved boy in church and the smartest boy in school. Here everyone expects me to be athletic and polite and, of course, *third.*" Mick snapped the hunk of bark he was holding and flung the pieces against a big tree root. "Sometimes I think I can't stand it. I feel like I'm being squeezed from all directions!"

"I feel like I'm being squeezed from all directions!"

"And you feel you're going to explode, just like that can of pop did when you dropped it on the driveway last night."

"Right! It's always pressure, pressure, pressure!"

"Hey, Mick," Flounder yelled. "Your turn to shoot."

Angel in My Backpack   *45*

"You take it," Mick yelled back.

Flounder shrugged his shoulders and walked back up to the firing line.

"You know, kid," Herbie said, sitting on a nearby toadstool, "pressure's nothing new. It's been around even longer than arrows and bulls-eyes. And it's not all bad, either. Pressure's an important part of ambition and achievement."

"But everybody expects too much from me!" Mick said, standing up and walking toward the archery range. "Why can't they just let me be *me* instead of some super boy who makes touchdowns with one hand and wins science projects with the other?"

"Remember what Audi said about tension?" Herbie asked.

Mick thought back to the first day of class. "Sure. He said that without it an arrow would never go anywhere."

"Tension in life is like that, too. It pushes you and lets you really accomplish things. The trick is to learn to *control* the tension and pressure you feel. Just the way you control the bow."

"Come on and shoot," Audi called to Mick.

Mick stepped up to the line and, as Audi called out commands, picked up his bow and shot. The arrow hit high on the stack of straw bales backing the target. His next two arrows were too low.

"Try a happy medium, kid," Herbie said. "Slow down and think about what you're doing. Feel the tension in the bow string."

Mick pulled. The string dug into his fingers, fighting against him. But with a final pull it gave way, and Mick could sense that he was in control. He raised his elbow high, held his breath, and fired. The arrow zinged into the bulls-eye with a solid thud.

"Another member for our BULLS-EYE CLUB!" Audi shouted.

At the close of the class, Mick sat on the sidelines

with the other boys and listened as Audi talked about archery. "Think only about what you're doing at that very moment. Don't waste energy worrying about what comes next."

Herbie whispered to Mick, "Good advice in life, too."

"And don't compare your shots with the person next to you," Audi went on. "Compare them to your own score the day before."

"Right!" Herbie said. "Be the best *you* can be—and be yourself."

"Finally," Audi said, "toughen up! Archery is a demanding sport."

"So is life!" Herbie flew up and looked Mick in the eye. "Growing up can be a real pain, kid. But God is always there to help."

Mick and Herbie walked back to the cabin. "Does the pressure get better, Herbie, once I'm all grown up?"

Herbie sighed. "No, not really. But you can learn to deal with it and even make it work for you. Just remember, it's important to lean on others sometimes and God *all* the time."

Mick looked at the BULLS-EYE CLUB certificate Audi had given him. "I'm going to keep this, Herbie, to remind me."

"Of your bulls-eye?"

Mick nodded. "And other things, too. That pressure isn't *all* bad, that I *can* learn to handle it."

"With some heavenly help," Herbie admonished.

"With some heavenly help," Mick said, as he and Herbie tacked the certificate above his bunk.

* * *

Cast all your anxiety on him [God] because he cares for you.
1 Peter 5:7

Day 11

The dining hall was decorated with bales of straw and lumpy, hand-stuffed scarecrows. Each table had a pink pig centerpiece, made from a milk jug.

"Welcome to 'Down on the Farm' night," K.C. said to Mick as he walked in the door. She wore bib overalls and her hair hung in braids over her shoulders. Fake freckles covered her face. "Y'all just sit down over yonder. The fried chicken'll be ready 'fore you know it." Then K.C. grinned, and Mick laughed to see both her front teeth were blacked out.

The campers had dressed for the occasion, wearing jeans and bandanas and straw hats. "This is my favorite 'theme night,'" Spike said, pulling a piece of straw from a bale and sticking it behind his ear.

The hopper bell rang and Jeff went to the kitchen for platters of fried chicken, homemade biscuits, and corn on the cob.

"Boy, that apple cobbler was good!" Varmint said later, licking his fork and placing it on his empty plate.

"Howdy!" Buckeye's voice rang out. "Now that y'all is finished with vittles, we'd like you to join us for the purtiest weddin' you ever seen. Just meet out by the flagpole in five minutes."

"I'm good at weddings," Paul said, sliding his plate across the table. "My dad's been married four times."

"My mom's been married twice," Jeff said.

"Everybody's mom's been married twice." Spike pushed his chair back from the table. "Let's get going."

Mick and his cabin mates were soon sitting on the grass, waiting to see what Buckeye had in store for them. Squirt was playing "Here Comes the Bride" on her harmonica. Cubbie came walking up from the stables, leading two horses. Dolly had a white veil on her head and a white satin garter on her leg. The horse beside her had a little black hat. A tie hung from his neck.

Buckeye appeared in a long black coat with a dandelion stuck in the top button hole. "Dearly beloved," he said, "we are gathered here to unite this horse and mare in holy matrimony. Do you, James ..." he began, but James took that moment to toss his head at a fly. "Is that a 'no'?" Buckeye asked. The campers all laughed. "How about you, Dolly? Do you take this horse to be your lawfully wedded ... uh ... husband?"

"I do," Cubbie said in a high voice, without moving his lips. James tossed his head again, knocking off his hat.

"All this excitement's just too much for him," Cubbie said. Dolly was pawing with her leg, trying to get the garter off. "Better hurry up this ceremony, Rev."

"By the power not invested in me by anybody," Buckeye finished, "I now pronouce you man and wife."

Angel in My Backpack

Cubbie pulled a handful of rice from his pocket and threw it on the horses. Everyone clapped and cheered.

"Well, that was a wedding with real class," Spike said as they walked back to their cabin.

"Yea. More than my dad's last wedding had," Paul mumbled from the back of the group.

"How about you, Mick?" Spike asked. "Have any stepparents to complain about?"

"No," Mick said. "Just one mom and one dad. They've been married for fifteen years."

"Wow!" Spike whistled. "You ought to call the *Guiness Book of World Records*. Nobody stays married that long anymore!"

"That's for sure," Paul said, his voice tight and low.

"I don't know why people even get married if they're just going to get divorced," Jeff said.

After lights out, Mick lay on his bunk. Herbie sat on the bottom rail, flossing his teeth with tiny gold string. "Why do people get married, Herbie?" Mick asked.

Herbie tucked away the string. "Well, love has a lot to do with it. And marriage is God's plan for mankind. When he created Adam, God realized that it wasn't good for man to be alone. So he caused a deep sleep to fall on Adam, and—"

"But nobody stays married anymore!" Mick interrupted. "You heard the guys talking. Everybody ends up unhappy and mad at each other. I'm never getting married."

"Don't be so hasty, kid. Sure, a lot of marriages fail. But it doesn't have to be that way. Some marriages are happy and fulfilling, where both partners love and care for one another. Look at your folks. And K.C.'s grandparents were happily married for over fifty years."

"But how can I be sure *my* marriage will be the happy kind, the kind that lasts?"

"It's tough to be sure of anything. Pray about your future partner. God has someone for you. Don't let yourself be trapped in a relationship by becoming too physical before marriage. Think about more than a girl's looks when you begin to date. And, most of all, remember the Golden Rule in dealing with a partner—whether it's your Saturday night date or your lifetime mate."

"You mean the Golden Rule we learned in Bible school years ago?"

"The very same. Matthew 7:12: 'Do to others what you would have them do to you,'" Herbie said. "Courtesy and kindness work wonders in a relationship—whether you're ten or twenty or sixty-two."

"Well," Mick said, rolling over on his stomach and closing his eyes. "Maybe I *will* get married. Someday."

"How do you feel about older women?" Herbie asked.

"Older women?"

"Uh-huh. I happen to know that K.C.'s birthday is two weeks before yours."

"Naw." Mick grinned. "I could never love a woman with no front teeth."

* * *

Marriage should be honored by all.
Hebrews 13:4

Day 12

"**D**on't forget to take bug spray," Varmint said. "Tonight we'll be invading *their* territory!"

Mick sprayed himself with insect repellent before he stuck it in the top of his backpack.

With Varmint in the lead, Mick's cabin trooped single file along the edge of camp to the trail leading through the pine forest. They went deeper and deeper, until they came to the campsite. A hand-painted sign on one of the trees read: "You have now entered Middle Earth. Take nothing but a memory; leave nothing but a footprint."

"Okay, men," Varmint said. "Drop your backpacks here by this tree and spread out to get firewood. We need two kinds of fuel: kindling—tiny twigs like this," he said, picking up pieces no thicker than toothpicks, "and larger pieces, some the size of pencils and others even bigger. Now get busy! We can't cook without a fire!"

Mick went a few feet into the forest and began picking up sticks. The voices of the other boys grew faint. The Christmas tree forest seemed to wrap him in its silence and peace. A rabbit skittered up and out of sight, its white tail bobbing like a bouncing ping-pong ball. Mick stood still and listened. All around him, tall trees bent and swayed with the wind. He could hear the *rat-tata-taa* of a woodpecker drilling for dinner.

Angel in My Backpack

"The idea is you bend over and pick up the sticks," Herbie said. "They won't just jump into your arms and volunteer to be kindling."

Mick smiled. "It's just so quiet here, Herbie. I'm hearing things I never heard before."

"Hear the river running down below the bank?"

Mick listened, and sure enough, a soft warble drifted up to him. "Wow," he said softly.

"What's really incredible, kid, is that these sounds are always here. It's just that no one hears them until he *listens* for them. Lots of things are like that."

"For instance?" Mick asked, loading his arms with twigs.

"You human beings talk to each other all the time, but you hardly ever really hear each other. Half the time one of you is busy thinking what he wants to say even while the other one is talking. And speaking from thousands of years of observation, I'd say that's a pretty common problem with humans."

"And angels don't have that problem?"

Herbie flew down and sat on Mick's shoulder. "What'd you say, kid? I wasn't listening."

"Not funny, Herbie."

Herbie laughed. "But the thing humans miss most by not listening is the voice of God."

Mick stopped and looked at Herbie. "God talks?"

"Of course God talks! Not like your principal when he makes Monday morning announcements and his voice booms into every room in the school. But God does speak. Right now he's talking to you through this chorus of his creation. And when you spend time alone with him, reading his word and talking to him, God speaks to you through his Holy Spirit."

"What does it sound like?"

"Sometimes the Holy Spirit shows you a special Bible verse to help you make a tough decision. Or to just make you feel happy in the Lord. Sometimes a still, small voice inside you will actually tell you just what you need to know, what you should do. And sometimes you will just feel the love of God so much, it's as though you've heard him say, 'Mick, I love you.'"

"Does everybody hear God's voice?" Mick asked, heading back toward camp with his armload of wood.

Herbie's wings drooped a bit. "No, kid, they don't. It's like the woosh of the wind or the warble of the lark. People who are listening for it, hear it."

"Hey, Mick!" Spike called. "We've already got the fire started. Bring that wood over here so we can get those 'hobo dinners' cooking!"

Soon the glowing coals were covered with misshapen hunks of foil, bulging with raw veggies and fresh meatballs.

After dinner, the boys sat on long logs arranged around the campfire. The smell of burning pine and moist earth filled the air. Varmint strummed songs on his guitar. "Time for bed," he said at last.

They all spread their sleeping bags around the campfire. The ground was a soft carpet made of layers and layers of pine needles. Mick zipped up his bag and lay watching the glowing embers of the fire. All was quiet. Mick looked up at stars peeking through feathery boughs. He listened.

"Good night, God," Mick whispered.

And a sudden swoosh of wind in the pines seemed to whisper back.

* * *

"Be still, and know that I am God."
Psalm 46:10

Day 13

Campers' voices filled the dining hall as they sang dinner's grace:

> Oh, the Lord is good to me,
> And so I thank the Lord
> For giving me the things I need—
> The sun, the rain, and the appleseed.
> The Lord is good to me.

"That 'Johnny Appleseed prayer' is my favorite one," Jeff said as the boys sat down and began to fill their plates with spaghetti.

"Why's it called that?" Mick said.

"Well," Spike said as he picked up the platter of warm breadsticks, "it's supposed to be the song Johnny Appleseed sang while he hiked across America planting apple trees. Can you imagine just wandering across the wilderness, doing what you wanted, when you wanted?"

"Sleeping under the stars every night. And eating M&M's three times a day if you wanted," Jeff said.

"Pass the butter," Varmint said. "And I don't think Johnny Appleseed carried any M&M's in his knapsack."

"I can't imagine that kind of freedom," Spike said. "My mom puts a leash on me when we go to the grocery store."

Mick grinned. "My mom's pretty protective, too."

"I can't wait to grow up," Paul said as he took the last breadstick.

"Any bug juice left?" Mick asked. Spike passed the big pitcher of fruit drink.

Half a dozen counselors began winding through the tables singing:

> We are, we are, we are
> the order of the oar.
> We are, we are, we are
> the order of the oar.
> Each and every one of us
> is sticking to the rest of us.
> We are, we are, we are
> the order of the oar.

Audi led the group and carried a big wooden oar. They stopped at one of the Buck tables where the younger boys ate. Mick stood up to get a better look and saw Preston.

"Is it *your* birthday?" the counselors all asked him. Preston pushed his glasses up on his nose and smiled.

"Stand up, please," Beaner said. Preston stood up.

"On the chair, please," Audi said, slapping the oar against his palm. Preston looked a little scared as he stood up on his chair.

Angel in My Backpack

"Bend over, please!" Beaner said.

Then each counselor took a turn giving Preston a pretend whack with the oar while all the other counselors "oohed" and "ouched." The whole dining hall sang "Happy Birthday" as K.C. brought out a birthday cake from the kitchen. It had blue roses on it and said "Happy Birthday Preston."

"His table gets cake. We get 'fruit mush,'" Spike said, taking some of the fruit cocktail and passing it.

"I remember when I was a Buck," Jeff said, picking out the cherries and eating them first. "I couldn't wait to be a Warrior."

"And now you can't wait to be an adult," Varmint said. "Better watch it, or you'll wish your whole life away."

"Mick." Mick looked up to see Preston standing beside him. "Here," Preston said as he plopped down a piece of birthday cake with a big rose on it and ran back to his table.

"Thanks!" Mick called, grabbing the cake before the other boys could swipe the frosting.

Mick finished eating his cake outside while he watched Flounder and Spike play tetherball. "Good cake?" Herbie inquired, as Mick licked the frosting off his fingers.

"Heavenly!"

"Well, I wouldn't go that far," Herbie said, wrinkling his nose. "Won't be long before you have a birthday yourself, kid."

"It can't be too soon for me," Mick said. "I wish I could age five years instead of one. I want to get my own car and a real money-making job. I want to vote for the next president of the United States. I want to fly to the moon, or find a cure for cancer, or maybe—"

"My, my," Herbie yawned. "You certainly are going to do marvelous things when you're all grown up. What about now?"

"Now?"

"Yes!" Herbie said, flying up to look Mick in the eye.

"Now, this very moment. Look around you and *live*. Don't spend so much time daydreaming about the future that you miss the present."

"But what can a kid do, really?"

"Don't sell yourself short. Josiah was eight years old when he became king of all Judah. Beethoven published his first piano sonatas when he was thirteen. And David was just about your age when he tangled with that ugly Goliath."

"I can't do any of those things, Herbie!" Mick said, standing up and brushing off the seat of his shorts.

"But there *are* things you can do. Opportunities for fun and friendship, chances to learn and grow—"

"Winner and still champion!" Flounder yelled as the tetherball swung around and onto the top of the pole. "Any new takers?" he asked as he unwound the ball. "It's the chance of a lifetime—"

"The opportunity of a lifetime, huh?" Mick asked, taking his stance opposite Flounder. "Sounds like just what I've been looking for."

Mick served; Flounder returned. Then Mick doubled up his fist and walloped the ball with all his might. It sailed around and around the pole—and up out of Flounder's reach.

Mick heard clapping and turned to see K.C. standing behind him. "Nice game," she said, smiling.

And suddenly Mick was glad—for tetherball and friendships and birthdays that come one year at a time.

* * *

Don't let anyone look down on you because you are young, but set an example for the believers in speech, in life, in love, in faith and in purity.

1 Timothy 4:12

Day 14

"Sure is warm today," Herbie said, fanning himself with his halo.

Mick wiped the sweat off his face with his shirt. "You're telling me! I can't wait to bite into that ice cream sandwich." Mick leaned around the boy in front of him. The line snaked up to the Trading Post, where Dave was handing out the afternoon treat.

Slowly, Mick moved forward. When he was near the front of the line, Iceman walked up. He patted the shoulder of the boy in front of Mick. "Thanks for saving my place," he said as he stepped in line.

"Hey, no cuts!" Mick said.

"I'm not cuttin'," Iceman said, pushing his sunglasses up on top of his head and turning around to face Mick. "I just had to go do something. But now I'm back." He poked Mick's chest with his finger. "And this is *my* place." Then he turned around.

Mick stood looking at the back of Iceman's neck, feeling his own redden with anger. Then he stepped out of line and slid in front of Iceman.

"Hey, what d'you think you're doing?" Iceman yelled.

"This is *my* place," Mick said without turning around.

"No way!" Iceman shoved Mick hard, and he fell to the ground beside the line.

Mick jumped to his feet and plowed into the side of

Iceman. Both boys went down. They rolled over and over, a mass of kicking legs and swinging arms.

"Fight!" somebody yelled. "It's a fight!"

Mick flung out his fist and felt the pain in his knuckles when they made contact with Iceman's jaw. The two wrestled in the dust, the faces above them a dizzying blur. Too late, Mick saw it coming. Iceman's fist smacked his eye with a loud, wet sound. But before Mick could land his next punch, a strong hand grabbed him by the arm and yanked him to his feet.

Iceman's fist smacked his eye with a loud, wet sound.

"That's enough!" Dave yelled. He held one boy with each hand. "What do you two think you're doing?" he demanded, shaking them the whole time. "Now get in my office!"

Later, Mick lay on his bunk, the ice pack the nurse had given him turning soggy against his swollen eye. "That's going to be a real beaut, kid." Herbie lifted the ice pack. "Black and blue already! I hear Iceman's pretty messed up, too."

Angel in My Backpack   61

"Who cares! I wish I could have *broken* his stupid jaw!"

"Just because he took cuts?"

"Don't lecture me, Herbie! What was I supposed to do, let him push me around forever?"

Herbie didn't answer right away, and a thick white silence seemed to fill the cabin.

"You humans and your *rights*!" Herbie said at last. "Always so afraid that someone will take advantage of you. When Christ was here on earth, the disciples he gathered around him never could understand his *gentle* strength. They couldn't understand that a man could have both courage *and* control. They kept waiting for Jesus to raise an army and cut the throats of the Roman soldiers." Herbie flew up in front of Mick, pacing the air and waving his arms. "And look at the way Christ died! Even though he had all authority in heaven and earth. You know what that means, kid?"

Mick shook his head.

"It means he could have called down lightning on the heads of his enemies or had them pulled limb from limb by a legion of angels! But instead he quietly and humbly died, so salvation could come to mankind. The weapons of Christ weren't words and fists; they were wisdom and love. Especially love."

"Even for his enemies?"

Herbie nodded. "The thing Christ kept trying to show his disciples was that it takes a lot more courage to stand for peace than it does to fall on the ground and punch and kick and grunt. *Anybody* can do that!"

Mick eased down off the bed. "But Iceman's such a creep, Herbie. He makes me feel like a real doormat every time he's around."

"No one can make you feel like a doormat unless you let him." Herbie said. "Standing up for your rights doesn't mean you have to settle things with your fists. In fact, knuckles never really settle anything. The world is full of

Icemen, and you can't break all their jaws! Besides, as a Christian you must bear the fruit of peace."

"Fruit of peace?"

"Galatians 5:22—'the fruit of the Spirit is peace.' That means the Holy Spirit will teach you how to get along with people who are pushy and obnoxious. How to use your head and heart to settle problems instead of your fists and feet."

"Even when that's hard to do?" Mick asked, picking up the ice pack.

"*Especially* when that's hard to do. You humans are such violent creatures! You've averaged one war every three years for over three thousand years!"

Mick walked toward the nurse's office to get a fresh ice pack. Herbie flew beside him. "Remember the Christmas cards your mom sent out last year?"

"Sure," Mick said. "I had to stuff them in the envelopes. The front had a picture of a lion and a lamb lying beside each other."

"And on the inside," Herbie continued, "the card read: 'Let there be peace on earth, and let it begin with me.' If every human being made that his prayer . . ."

Mick paused with his hand on the door of the nurse's cabin. "Would that really make a difference, Herbie?"

Herbie shrugged his shoulders, his wings lifting lightly. "It just might."

Mick went on inside, while Herbie waited on the porch. "Who knows, kid," Herbie said to himself. "With some real effort maybe you—and Iceman and Spike and everybody else—can change those gruesome statistics on war. One fight at a time."

* * *

Make every effort to live in peace with all men.

Hebrews 12:14

Angel in My Backpack

Day 15

hy do we have to stay on our beds during rest hour?" Spike complained, sitting cross-legged on his bunk and throwing a ping-pong ball against the wall. "I want to go swimming."

"The same reason we have to turn out lights at 10 P.M. and get up at 7 A.M. Rules," Jeff said.

"Why don't you guys just shut up so those of us who *want* to rest *can!*" Paul said as he buried his head under his pillow.

"Hey, guys," Varmint said. "This is Tuesday—and that means you need to write your folks. If you need paper or stamps, let me know."

"Another dumb rule," Spike said as he reached for his notebook.

Mick lay on his stomach, chewing on the eraser end of his pencil. Blank, wide-lined paper stared at him. He wrote:

Dear Mom,

"Catchy beginning, kid. I like it," Herbie said from the foot of the bed.

"I hate writing letters. Everything I say sounds dumb."

"Believe me, your mom *loves* your letters. She reads each one about a zillion times.

Mick lowered his head and began writing.

Angel in My Backpack

How are you? I am fine. It is hot here. We swim a lot. I went on a mud hike. Don't worry about the clothes I wore. I never liked that outfit anyway. The food is okay. Except this morning we had oatmeal. I hate oatmeal, but you already know that.

"Tell her about the kite flying," Herbie prompted.
"Yeah!" Mick said. "That was fun!"

Yesterday we flew kites. Every camper had one. They were all different. Mine was purple. We flew them on the playing fields around Mt. Wood. A big oak tree grabbed Flounder's. (He's this guy I know.) Mine got so high I could barely see it. And the wind pulled and pulled on the string. It took me almost an hour to wind it back down. I better go now. They make us write letters every Tuesday. But I probably would have written anyway.

> *Love,*
> *Mick*

Herbie flew up out of Mick's backpack with a stamp. "Thanks," Mick said, licking the stamp and sticking it on the corner of the envelope. Then he stretched out and closed his eyes.

"Those kites were really something," Herbie said.
"Yeah," Mick said. "Sometimes I thought my string would break for sure!"
"You know, kid, rules are sort of like kite strings."
Mick opened his eyes. "Rules like kite strings? That sounds weird even for you, Herbie."
"Boundaries, rules. They're all important."
"They're all a drag."
"That, too, sometimes." Herbie smiled. "But necessary. People are like kites—they need limitations to keep them from soaring out of sight, from crashing into each other. To remind them of responsibilities. To teach them self-control and discipline."
"So who holds my 'string'?" Mick asked.
"Lots of people right now. Teachers, parents,

counselors; your principal and your pastor and your coach. These 'string holders' are the authority figures in your life, the rule-makers."

"Will they ever let go of the string? Ever let me do what I want?"

"Sooner than you think, you'll be grown up. But there *is* someone who'll always hold on to your string. No matter what."

Mick looked at Herbie. "God?"

"God. He'll always be there, kid. No matter how high you climb. No matter how hard you fall."

"Okay," Varmint said, rolling off his bunk. "Rest hour's over. Let's go by the mailbox and deposit our letters. Then we'll challenge those wimpy Warrior girls to a game of kickball."

The boys laced on their shoes and grabbed their letters. They were on the front porch of the cabin when Mick asked, "Hey, where's Spike?"

And they all looked back to see Spike still on his bunk, fast asleep.

* * *

Whoever gives heed to instruction prospers, and blessed is he who trusts in the Lord.

Proverbs 16:20

Day 16

Mick walked between the rows of log seats, looking for litter—his cabin's assignment for the day. "Here, kid, you missed this." Herbie flew up from under the bleachers with a gum wrapper.

"Thanks."

"What'd you think of chapel today?"

"It was okay."

"Only okay?"

Mick sat down and kicked at some dead leaves near his feet. "I guess I'm just sick of everybody telling me how great it is to be a Christian. Of everybody telling me to be good, good, good."

"There are worse things you could be than good," Herbie said.

"There are better things, too!"

"Like popular?"

"Maybe," Mick said. He crunched leaves under the soles of his shoes. "The truth is, Herbie, I don't want to be a 'goody-goody.' I want to be like everyone else. We had this kid in our school last year who carried a big black Bible everywhere. The kids all laughed at him and called him 'preacher.' I don't want to be a Christian if it means doing that! And some grownup's always telling me about all the things a Christian teen *shouldn't* do. What fun is it if you can't be one of the guys?"

Angel in My Backpack

"Listen, kid," Herbie said, settling himself on the bleacher opposite Mick. "Being a Christian doesn't mean you grow two heads or turn into some kind of side-show freak. It simply means you give your heart to Jesus and let him take control of your life. It means you have joy and peace, not some awful disease that keeps you from enjoying life. And being a Christian will save you from a lot of hurt and regret."

"But I'll have to be different from the other kids, won't I?"

"Sure, in some ways. The way of the world is selfish. The way of Christ is *selfless*. That doesn't mean you go around wearing a 'kick me' sign. It simply means that you realize you're not the most important person in the world, that other people have needs and rights, too."

"Sounds like 'I Am Third' again."

"The way of the world is, 'If it feels good, do it.' The way of Christ is to live above that, to think about consequences and commitments. The way of the world is paved with heartbreak; the way of Christ is filled with hope."

"But I'm afraid I can't do it, Herbie. I don't think I can be a Christian when the other guys are drinking or cheating or cussing or taking drugs."

Herbie flew down and picked up a crumpled, brown leaf. "See this oak leaf?"

"Of course I see that oak leaf!"

"Oak leaves can be very stubborn things. In the fall, when every other leaf lets go and swirls to the ground, some oak leaves hold on tight. All through the icy months of winter they cling to the branches. The oak tree sleeps while these few determined leaves hang on through blizzards and biting cold. But in the spring, the oak tree stretches itself and prepares for a new batch of leaves. Sap courses through the trunk and limbs. Tiny buds begin to form. And then those old leaves are pushed off. Not so much by external forces as by internal power."

70   *Day 16*

"So?" Mick said.

"So," Herbie continued, "it's that way with being a Christian. The new life Christ gives you will push off the things of the world, just like the tree pushed off this leaf. And the closer you stay to God, the more you communicate with him, the more you listen to him—the easier it is to be a Christian. And the more fun life will be!"

Mick looked up at the chapel cross, made from big, rough logs. *Dear Jesus,* he prayed, *you know that deep down I really do want to be a Christian. But sometimes, well, I'm a real coward about it. Give me courage, God. So I will want to be like you, instead of like everybody else.*

Herbie flew up to sit on Mick's shoulder. "And now we'd better get going, or we'll be late for that softball game."

"Softball," Mick smiled. "Now there's a game where I AM THIRD is really true."

"Why?"

"Because," Mick laughed as he ran back toward camp, "I am third baseman!"

* * *

Therefore, if anyone is in Christ, he is a new creation; the old has gone, the new has come!

2 Corinthians 5:17

Day 17

$\mathbb{M}$ick closed his eyes. "Three types of water rescues are drag, hair carry, and ... and ..."

"Cross-chest carry," Herbie said.

Mick opened his eyes. "What's the use! I'll *never* be able to remember all this stuff for the lifesaving test this afternoon." He tossed the book aside and rolled over on his back. "Hopeless, Herbie. Totally hopeless!"

"Let me help you review, kid." Herbie opened the book. "Now, when throwing a ring buoy, where should the rescuer aim?"

"Directly behind the victim."

Herbie turned a few pages. "Ah, here's a good question. What is the best way to protect yourself from aquatic predators?"

"Don't swim where they might be."

Herbie laughed. "Sounds like information Jonah could have used." He leafed over to the next chapter. "What do you call the sudden unreasoning and overwhelming terror that destroys a person's capacity for self-help?"

Mick sat up. "Boy, do I know that answer! *Panic.* I've got plenty of that—only mine's not unreasonable, just overwhelming. How can they expect a guy to remember all this stuff? And even if I could pass the written test, I still have to rescue three victims from the deep end of the pool. I must have been crazy to ever think I could become a lifeguard!"

Herbie closed the lifesaving manual and looked at Mick. "One last question. What's the number one water safety rule?"

"Simple. Never swim alone."

"And why not?"

"Because if you run into trouble, there's no one to help you."

"You know, kid, you're not alone when it comes to taking this lifesaving test, either."

"You mean I have *you*?"

Herbie shook his head. "I mean *God*."

"Come on," Mick said. "I'm sure God has more important things to worry about than whether or not I pass this crummy lifesaving test! I mean, people are starving—"

"Believe me, kid, your problem is as important to God as anything on earth."

"You've got to be kidding! What difference does it make to God whether or not I'm a lifeguard?"

Herbie flew over to Mick's backpack. "I know another manual that might help you." He pulled out Mick's Bible. "Look at Isaiah 63:9."

Mick turned to the place. "In all their distress he too was distressed."

Angel in My Backpack

"You see, kid, God is concerned with *everything* that concerns you. Nothing is too big; nothing is too small. He knows how much you've studied, how scared you are, how important this is to you. And that makes it important to him, too."

"I never thought God cared much about little stuff."

"Little stuff is his specialty! God wants to help you be the best you can be. That's what Proverbs 3:5 means."

Mick leafed back to Proverbs. "Trust in the Lord with all your heart and lean not on your own understanding."

"It's your job to study and try hard. It's God's job to help you do your best."

"Does that mean I'll pass the test?"

"It means," Herbie said, opening the lifesaving manual and handing it to Mick, "that you have a few more hours before class—and God expects you to use them studying instead of groaning about how impossible that test will be!"

Mick bent over his book and began reading. "The most important thing a victim needs is trust in his lifeguard."

"Trust is pretty important *for* lifeguards, too," Herbie said, leaving the Bible on Mick's pillow for later.

* * *

I can do everything through him who gives me strength.

Philippians 4:13

Angel in My Backpack

Day 18

Mick hurried across the grass, the morning dew making squeaky, wet sounds under his tennis shoes. A chill tinged the air and a mist hung over the pool. "I think I regret this already," Mick mumbled through a yawn, pulling up the hood of his sweatshirt.

From across the lawn, other Polar Bears were coming out of their cabins. "Hey, gang!" Flounder called and waved. "Love these frosty dips!"

The campers all kicked off their shoes, ducked into the locker rooms for quick showers, and stood hesitantly around the pool. Dave walked out of the office, wearing jogging pants and a T-shirt with a big polar bear on it. "All right, Polar Bears, time for your morning swim. On the count of three. Three!" Plunks and splashes and squeals filled the air as the campers plunged into the water.

"Hey!" Mick said, treading water in the deep end. "It's warm. The water is warm!" Mick looked over to see Preston sitting on the side of the pool, wrapped in his towel and shivering. "Preston!" Mick yelled. "Come on in! The water's warm."

"N-n-no, thanks," Preston said, his teeth chattering.

Flounder climbed out of the pool and stood dripping on the cement next to Preston. "So how are things with the Bucks?" he asked as he sat down and pulled on his shirt.

Preston shrugged. "Okay, I guess."

"Taken any scalps lately?"

Preston grinned. "Uh-uh."

"Well, when the Great Flounder here was a Buck . . ."

"Don't bore the kid," Spike said, splashing water on Flounder. "When you were a Buck you were a wimpy, homesick thing."

"Really?" Preston asked, looking up at Flounder.

Flounder laughed. "Yep. Sad but true. I wasted my whole first week at camp crying and begging to call home."

"But he's been coming back every summer since," Spike said as he climbed out of the pool and sat on the other side of Preston. "Camp Kickapoo couldn't be Camp Kickapoo without Flounder."

"Why do they call you Flounder?" Preston asked.

"Don't ask!" Mick laughed as he dog-paddled over to them, keeping only his head above the water.

Flounder stood up and pulled off his T-shirt. His belly hung in little pockets over his swim trunks.

"Ladies and gentlemen," Spike yelled through cupped hands, "we present for your enjoyment a feat never before equaled in the history of the world. The Great Flounder and his amazing belly waves!"

Angel in My Backpack

Suddenly Flounder's belly began to move. It rippled up and down, like melty Jell-O. Preston watched wide-eyed as the belly waves continued. Finally Flounder started to giggle and doubled over in laughter. "It tickles after a while," he said.

By the time Mick got back to the cabin, he felt as though even his bones were shivering. He stepped into a hot shower before dressing for breakfast. Then he went out on the porch to wait for Varmint and the others.

"So how do you like being a Polar Bear?" Herbie asked, sitting on the porch rail and dangling his feet over the side.

"It's okay," Mick said. "But when you come out of that water, you wish you really *did* have a furry, white coat to keep you warm."

"Polar Bears don't exactly have white fur," Herbie said. Mick looked at him. "Oh, yeah?"

"I mean it! A polar bear's fur is made up of thousands of tiny, transparent strands. They look so white because they're surrounded by white—snow and glaciers and ice caps. In the summer they turn yellowish so they blend in with the melting ice."

"Is this on the level, Herbie?"

"Certainly! Lots of creatures have the ability to blend in with their surroundings. Remember the chameleon Andy brought to school last year?"

Mick laughed. "It turned whatever color we put it on— green if it was on a leaf and red when we put it on Mrs. Miles' gradebook."

"Chameleons are interesting little beasts," Herbie said. "But they get zero points for individuality. Kind of reminds me of some humans I've known."

"What do you mean by that?"

"Some people spend their whole lives trying to look like everybody else and dress like everybody else and talk like everybody else. And you know what happens to them in the end, kid?" Mick shook his head. "They end up being no one at all—just a shadow of everybody else. And God really hates that, because he *loves* individuality."

"Really?"

"Sure!" Herbie said, flying up and waving his arms as he talked. "That's why roses are pink and daisies are white and petunias are both. That's why birds chirp and hyenas laugh and people talk. That's why Spike has freckles and Paul has brown eyes and you have blond hair. That's why Flounder can do belly waves and K.C. can play the piano. That's why Buckeye sings so well and Dave swims like a fish and Beaner's so good at climbing Mt. Wood."

Mick started down the steps toward the dining hall. "I've decided, Herbie. I'm going to start being more of an individual. I'm going to start doing more what I want to do instead of just trying to blend in with the crowd."

"'Atta boy," Herbie said, slapping Mick on the shoulder. "Be your own man!"

"And you know when I'm going to start all this individuality stuff?" Mick grinned.

"When?"

"Tomorrow morning—by sleeping late. I hate being a Polar Bear!"

* * *

God saw all that he had made, and it was very good.
Genesis 1:31

Day 19

Mick and K.C. sat in the shade of a big maple tree, watching the Warrior pillow fights.

"Get 'em!" Spike screamed. "The knees! Go for the knees, Jeff!"

Jeff and Susan stood on tires with their feet wide apart, bracing themselves for the whacks and thunks and thuds of combat. Varmint blew his whistle, and the contest was on. Jeff and Susan swung blindly, while their cheering sections screamed out strategies. Susan toppled a little, but kept her feet firm and tried to regain her balance.

"Again!" Spike yelled. "Hit her again!"

Just as Susan fell off the tire, Jeff's pillow burst. Fluffy white feathers drifted onto the ground. A playful breeze grabbed handfuls and flung them across the grass.

"Looks like snow," Mick laughed.

"When I was little," K.C. said, "I used to visit my grandparents every Christmas. Sometimes it would snow these huge, fluffy flakes. And Grandpa would take me in his lap and say, 'Look, the angels are having pillow fights!' But I would shake my head and tell him that angels were too well-behaved for stuff like that."

At that very moment, Herbie drifted by, his halo stuffed with feathers. "How!" he said to Mick. "Me Chief Pale Pillow, heap big Injun." He gave a war whoop and dove after more feathers.

"I don't know," Mick said. "Maybe angels aren't quite as well-behaved as you think. Tell your grandpa I agree with him!"

K.C. stared down at a clover blossom growing near her feet. "He died. Grandpa died."

Mick felt his cheeks flush. "Gee, I didn't know. I mean, I'm sorry."

"That's okay. It was a heart attack. And he died."

The pillow fighting had started again, with the boys' and girls' cabins cheering new contestants.

Mick didn't know what to say. K.C. sat watching the pillow fights, her eyes sad, her fingers touching that single wooden bead she wore on a leather string around her neck. Mick had seen a few other campers wear the same kind.

"Nice necklace," Mick said. "Was it a craft project?"

"Are you kidding? This is my Sagamore bead."

"Your what-a-more bead?" Mick asked.

"Sagamore. It's the Indian word for 'leader.' To be chosen as Sagamore is the biggest honor you can get at Camp Kickapoo."

"So how do you get chosen?" Mick asked. "Be the camper with the most mosquito bites or the biggest patches of poison ivy?"

K.C. smiled. "No. To be worthy of Sagamore, one must truly live the 'I Am Third' motto. Counselors decide on just a few campers each session who will get this honor. No one knows who's been picked till closing campfire. The ceremony is real neat. And real serious. Me and Spike both made Sagamore last year." She was quiet for a minute. "Grandpa would have been proud of me."

A bumble bee buzzed heavily over the clump of nearby clover. The sounds of the pillow fight seemed muffled by the afternoon heat. Mick tried to think of something to say.

"Look, a snowflake," K.C. said, picking up a feather that landed beside her foot. "And here's another one." Several more feathers drifted down in front of her. "It really *is* snowing feathers!" she laughed, snatching at the white pieces.

Mick looked up. Herbie hovered overhead, plucking his halo headpiece and dropping them into K.C.'s lap.

"Grandpa must've been right about the angels' pillow fights," she said, running the fluffy edges of a feather across her cheek. "He was always right."

"You miss him, don't you?" Mick asked.

"Uh-huh. A lot. My mom says I'll see him again. Someday. She says he's waiting for us all in heaven." K.C. turned and looked Mick in the eye. "Think she's right?"

"I guess so. Sure," Mick said.

"Tell her heaven's a swell place," Herbie said, settling onto Mick's shoulder.

"And heaven's a swell place," Mick said.

"Tell her about the streets of gold and gates of pearl."

"All the streets are made of pure gold," Mick said. "And the gates of pearl."

"Really?" K.C. said.

"Tell her best of all there's no pain or sadness—and that God himself fills the whole place with light," Herbie said.

But before Mick could say anything, K.C. asked, "Suppose Grandpa's happy there, with all that fancy stuff?"

"Oh, sure!" Mick said. "Because there's never any pain or sadness. And God's love lights up the whole place."

K.C. looked closely at Mick. "How come you know so much about heaven?"

"Well—you could say a friend told me."

"Sure it wasn't a little bird that told you?" K.C. laughed as she stood up to take her turn at pillow fighting.

Herbie began to flap his arms and fly around in circles.

"Maybe it *was* a bird after all," Mick said, swatting at Herbie. Herbie laughed.

K.C. looked around. "Did you hear that?"

"Hear what?" Mick asked as they picked up their pillows and walked toward the group.

"I thought I heard windchimes."

"Maybe you did." Mick laughed as he picked a feather out of her hair. "Or maybe it was just one of the angels laughing—because we humans like having pillow fights, too!"

* * *

"I [Jesus] am the resurrection and the life. He who believes in me will live, even though he dies."

John 11:25

Angel in My Backpack

Day 20

The plastic water slide lay on the hill like a fat, blue snake. Beaner stood at the top, hosing it down. Below, Varmint and Audi were busy placing bales of straw at the far end to make sure no one ran into any trees.

"And who's going to be first this year?" Beaner said, smiling.

Spike stepped aside and pushed Mick to the front of the line. "Mick is."

"Gee, thanks," Mick said. "I think." He handed Spike his towel and lay down on his stomach at the top of the slide.

"Push off with your hands," Beaner said.

Mick began to slip down the wet plastic. The water was cold on his stomach and lapped at his ribs as he started to pick up speed. He began to go faster. And faster. The slide felt like a wet ribbon drawn across him. The bales of straw seemed to get bigger as he sped toward them. Just before he crashed, Mick began to slow down and was able to pull himself up on all fours.

"How was it?" Spike yelled.

"Excellent!" Mick laughed, standing up and trying to catch his breath.

Within an hour, Mick had learned to go down on his back and even on his knees. Twice he was able to go so far that he crashed into the straw.

"Did you hear about Iceman?" Flounder asked as they stood in line.

"What about him?" Mick said.

"They may make him go home. Dave found cigarettes in his suitcase."

"I heard it was a joint of marijuana," Jeff said.

"Why would anyone have that stuff at camp?" Mick asked.

"Why would anyone have that stuff at all!" Flounder huffed.

"Big deal," Paul said. "Lots of adults smoke and drink. And they take drugs a lot worse than grass. Besides, my dad says a little won't hurt you."

"Then your dad's a jerk," Flounder said, stepping up to take his turn on the water slide.

"He is not!" Paul yelled. "You're just scared to try stuff like that. You're just a big baby!"

Flounder pushed off and whizzed down the water slide without looking back.

The boys were playing tetherball that evening when they saw a big, black car pull away from the lodge, driven by an angry-looking lady with bright yellow hair. Iceman sat in the passenger seat. Dave stood watching them drive away.

Angel in My Backpack

"Why does everybody get so upset when kids want to try a few things?" Paul asked, hitting the ball with his fist.

"You mean like cigarettes and joints and booze?" Flounder grabbed the ball. "You gotta be crazy to use that stuff, man! One beer leads to a six-pack—and then you've got to try the hard stuff. Soon you're stuck with a habit and a hangover every morning. And it's even worse with drugs!"

"My mom *has* to have her cigarettes," Spike said. "Her hands shake like crazy if she's late for a dose of that nicotine."

"I smoked a joint once," Paul said.

The boys were quiet for a moment. "How was it?" Jeff asked.

Paul shrugged his shoulders. "It made me feel funny."

Flounder picked up a handful of pebbles and began throwing them on the driveway. "I'm telling you—that stuff will kill you!"

Paul half laughed. "Hey, it's *my* body."

"You start out with a little and think you know what you're doing—but before you know it, you're not the one in charge," Flounder said. "And you end up doing all kinds of stuff just to get a drink or a fix."

"Like the water slide," Mick said.

"The water slide? That's stupid!" Paul snorted.

"Well," Mick said, "up at the top you start out slow and in control, but soon you're zooming down that hill lickety-split, going faster and faster, until sometimes you have to crash into the bales of straw to stop. You start messing with drugs—"

"And the crash-ups can be pretty awful," Flounder said, his voice hoarse and soft.

Later that night, Mick sat on the porch reading his Bible while the other boys finished their showers. A soft glimmer appeared on the rail and soon Herbie was sitting beside Mick. "Too bad about Iceman," Herbie said. "I liked what you said about the water slide. You get much smarter, kid, and you won't need me at all."

"I'll always need you, Herbie."

Herbie hovered in front of Mick. "You know what Paul said today, about how it was his body and if he wanted to mess it up it was his business?" Mick nodded. "Well, that's not exactly true. Look at 1 Corinthians 6:19-20."

Mick opened his Bible to the passage and read, " 'Do you not know that your body is a temple of the Holy Spirit, who is in you, whom you have received from God? You are not your own; you were bought at a price. Therefore honor God with your body.' "

"You see, kid, your body's not really your own. It, along with your heart and life, belongs to God. When Christ died on the cross, he paid the price for all of you. And he doesn't want you to mess up his merchandise with black lungs or a rotten liver or a few thousand dead brain cells."

Flounder came out and sat down beside Mick. For a minute neither boy spoke. "Wonder what Iceman's doing right now?" Mick said.

Flounder shrugged his shoulders. "Who knows," he sighed. "Last year . . . my brother—he almost died of an overdose. And he was only sixteen." Flounder bit his lower lip. "Dumb. It was just plain dumb."

"No wonder you hate drugs so much!" Mick said.

The porch light flickered. "Lights out, guys!" Varmint called. Mick and Flounder barely made it to their bunks before Varmint flipped the switch and darkness settled on the cabin.

Outside, Herbie leafed through his spiral notebook until he came to Mick's spot. "You're learning fast, kid," he said, placing another gold star on the almost-full page.

*   *   *

Those who belong to Christ Jesus have crucified the sinful nature with its passions and desires.

Galatians 5:24

Angel in My Backpack

Day 21

Dave supervised the stacking of the canoes on the trailer. When the last one had been secured, he said, "All aboard! Next stop—up river!"

The campers piled on the big, orange bus for the seven-mile ride upstream, where they would put their canoes in and float back to camp. The bus pulled out of camp, with the load of canoes following along like a pyramid of waddling baby ducks.

"Easy now!" Dave cautioned as they unloaded the canoes. "And everybody has to wear a PFD."

"A what?" Mick asked Spike.

"A 'personal flotation device,'" Spike said. "It's just a fancy word for lifejacket."

Three boys were assigned to each canoe. "Remember, the guy in the back does the steering," Dave said. "Watch out for rocks and tree limbs. And if your canoe drags bottom, get out right away and wade through. Have fun— and I'll see you back at camp."

Mick saw Preston standing at the edge of the water. His big PFD made his arms and legs look toothpick thin. "Hey, Preston," Mick called as he walked over to him. "You like canoeing?"

Preston looked at the gray water. "Long as we don't tip." He pushed his glasses up on his nose. "Do you think we'll tip?"

Angel in My Backpack

Mick tightened the straps on Preston's life jacket. "Probably not, but there's no way you can sink with this thing on!" He gave Preston's PFD a few playful punches.

Audi and Varmint helped launch each canoe. "Keep those PFD's on at all times!" Varmint yelled as he and Audi climbed into their own canoe and slithered out into the river.

Flounder was in back and Mick had the front position. Spike sat in the middle. "Look at this stuff," Spike said as he scooped up a handful of water. "It's the color of dirty Army fatigues."

"Rock ahead!" Mick yelled. In the center of the river, water was breaking around a huge boulder.

"Looks like it's swimming upstream," Flounder laughed as they steered around it.

The canoes in front of them drifted on downstream. Suddenly the air was pierced with squeals and screams. "What happened?" Flounder asked, trying to see around Spike.

"Somebody's canoe tipped," Mick said. Out in the water, several boys bobbed around like huge oranges. Mick strained to see. Preston!

"Paddle!" Mick yelled back to Flounder. By the time they reached the spot, Audi had helped right the canoe. Mick saw Preston sitting in the stern, shivering. "You okay?" Mick yelled across.

Preston nodded his head. "Yeah—I think so."

"I hate tipping," Flounder said, looking at the soaked campers. "Every time it happens, I feel like some huge orange turtle trying to climb back into the canoe." He laid down his paddle. "Let's just float for a while."

The only sounds were water bumping their canoe and an occasional peal of laughter from the canoes ahead of them. Mick looked up to see Herbie sitting on the bow of the canoe.

"No one's allowed on board without a PFD." Mick grinned.

"Right here," Herbie said, fluttering his wings.

"I'm sure glad Preston had his PFD on when they tipped," Mick said. "Poor kid was scared to death."

"And the place they swamped was one of the spots in the river where it's too deep to touch bottom. Without it he could have been in real trouble."

"No wonder Varmint told us we had to wear these the whole time we were on the water!"

Herbie flew up and sat next to Mick. "Your other PFD, of course, is worn *all* the time—wherever you are."

"What other PFD?"

"The PFD of God's love," Herbie said, shooing a dragonfly off his halo. "It's God's love for you that holds you up—no matter what happens to you. It's his love that keeps you from sinking into sin. His love is with you in hard, as well as happy, times. And it's God's love that keeps you afloat, even when the situation seems hopeless. Even when you can't touch bottom."

"We'd better paddle for a while," Flounder called from the back of the canoe.

The dragonfly was back, circling Herbie's head and coming in for a landing. "Pesky beast!" Herbie said, taking a swipe at him. He swooped in close and tried to nibble on Herbie's wings.

"You'd better scram, Herbie," Mick laughed as he picked up his paddle, "before *your* PFD becomes *his* dinner."

"What'd you say?" Spike asked, yawning and sitting up.

"Oh, nothing. Just that I'm sure glad for my PFD." Mick looked at Herbie. "Both of them!" he whispered.

* * *

**The Lord's unfailing love surrounds the
man who trusts in him.**

Psalm 32:10

Angel in My Backpack

Day 22

Mick walked toward the laundry hut, quarters jingling in his pocket, a pillowcase full of dirty clothes thrown over his shoulder. He had gotten up extra early so he could get a washer and dryer before the place buzzed with sweaty campers washing mounds of muddy, grimy clothes.

The laundry hut was empty. "All right!" Mick said, emptying his pillowcase into first one washer and then the other.

Herbie held his nose. "Phew! I think this batch ripened a little too long! What stinks so much?"

Mick held up a slimy gray object. "Mud hike clothes." Mick got the big box of soap powder off the shelf in the corner. He dumped some into the open top of each washer. "These things are pretty dirty," he said. "Maybe a little more." He poured in more soap. "Just a little gets your whole wash clean," Mick read on the back of the box.

"I'm not sure it was *your* wash the ad man had in mind when he wrote that, kid," Herbie said.

"You're right," Mick said, bringing the box back and opening the two washers. "If a little is good, imagine what a lot will do."

"I don't know . . ."

But before Herbie could say anything more, Mick piled mounds of soap into each machine. Then he shoved in his quarters. "There, that should do it. Come on, Herbie. Let's shoot a few baskets while these things wash."

Later, when he started back to check on his clothes, Mick saw a crowd of campers gathered outside the laundry hut. When he got closer, he couldn't believe his eyes. Huge mountains of white rolled out the door, making frothy rivers that ran in all directions.

"Oh, no!" Mick yelled, breaking into a run. When he got to the laundry hut, he pushed his way through the group of laughing kids and struggled to get in the door. "My clothes!"

"Hey, Mick!" someone yelled. "Think you used enough soap?" Everybody laughed.

"Mr. Clean to the rescue!" another camper shouted. "Go, Mr. Clean!"

"Mr. Clean to the rescue!" another camper shouted. "Go, Mr. Clean!" The crowd joined in, "Go, Mr. Clean!"

Inside, the whole place looked as if it had been sprayed with whipped cream. The washers were still churning, burping bubbles and making deep grating sounds.

"Herbie, what should I do?"

"Start by pushing that big round dial and turning them off," Herbie yelled down as he drifted by on a huge bubble.

Mick did, and the washers wound down like tired tops. The whole laundry hut smelled of detergent. From outside came squeals of laughter as kids pelted each other with soapsuds. "Hey, Mr. Clean," someone called, "wanna do my laundry next?"

"Dumb, dumb, dumb!" Mick groaned.

"What a mess!" said a voice. Mick looked up to see Dave standing in the doorway, a deep frown on his face. "Here," he said, shoving a mop and bucket toward Mick. "And don't leave until this mess is *completely* cleaned up."

It took Mick almost two hours to do the laundry hut. He had to mop and mop and mop the floor until all the suds were gone. Then he had to rinse everything with clear water. Twice.

Finally, he made it back to the cabin with his clothes. The other guys were gone to classes, but there—on his bunk—was a bar of soap and a sign that said: "Mr. Clean Lives Here." "Very funny," Mick said, knocking both to the floor. He dumped out his dry clothes and began folding them. "How many times did I mop that stupid laundry hut, Herbie?"

"You don't want to know, kid."

"I've never been so embarrassed in all my life! All I wanted were clean clothes."

"You know, kid . . ."

"Don't do it, Herbie!" Mick said, turning and shaking a pair of freshly folded socks at Herbie. "If you tell me 'the moral of this story is' I swear I'll wrap your halo around your neck!"

"Okay, okay! No need for violence. I'll just brush my teeth while you cool off." Herbie pulled out his gold toothbrush and flew to the bathroom. When he came out, Mick was lying on his bunk, tearing the "Mr. Clean" sign into tiny strips.

"Besides," Mick said, as if the conversation had never been interrupted, "there *is* no lesson to be learned from this disaster. Except maybe to measure the detergent next time I do laundry."

"Whatever you say, kid," Herbie said, leafing through an open comic book lying on Spike's bed.

The air was thick and quiet. Mick jumped off his bed. "Go ahead! Say it, Herbie!"

"Say what?" Herbie asked as he looked up.

"I know you're just dying to tell me something!"

Herbie laughed. His gold teeth glistened in the sunshine. "Only that more is not always better."

"You mean as in soap?"

"I mean as in lots of things. Baseball, television, telephone conversations. Pizza, sleep, weight lifting."

"What are you talking about, Herbie?"

"Look, kid, the key to success in life is moderation. Learning to stay away from extremes—whether in jogging or junk food. And the soap powder disaster helped teach you an important truth: more is not always better. A little salt makes popcorn tasty; a lot of salt makes popcorn trash. Part of growing up is knowing when enough really *is* enough."

"Why does life have to be so embarrassing, Herbie?" Mick said as he slipped the fresh case on his pillow.

Herbie pulled a leftover bubble from behind his back. "That's part of growing up, too, kid," he said, tossing the blue-green bubble to Mick, who popped it between his palms with a firm, wet *whack*.

* * *

The man who fears God will avoid all extremes.
Ecclesiastes 7:18

Day 23

It was time for the final Field Day event—the mile run. And, as usual, Audi's cabin was in the lead. "Why don't we just forget this event," he said, "so me and my boys can start the victory celebration!"

"Field Day isn't over yet!" Varmint said.

"It might as well be," Audi smirked. "Your cabin will have to take first place to win, and I know they can't do it."

"Oh, yeah?" Spike yelled. "Well you just watch Mick! We call him Quick Mick because he's so fast!"

Audi laughed and walked away.

"Quick Mick?" Mick groaned as he stretched out for the race.

"I had to think of something," Spike shrugged.

"Just do your best," Varmint said, walking Mick to the starting line. "But if you can pull this one off, you'll make me the happiest counselor in the whole world! Audi's cabin has taken first place for the last five years. The banner's been over his bunk so long he thinks he owns it!"

"Remember," Dave said, "the orange cones mark the route. Stay inside the orange cones. Now—on your mark, get set, go!" A crack of the starting gun, and the race was on. The runners sprinted down the path and disappeared into the woods.

Minutes passed. Then, through a break in the trees, the pack of runners appeared. "They're coming!"

"Who's in the lead?" Jeff asked.

"Stand back, fellas," Dave said as he stepped up to the finish line.

The runners rounded a bend and headed out of the woods. "It's Mick!" Spike yelled. "Mick's in the lead!"

Mick pushed himself toward the finish line, stretching his stride to stay ahead. Behind him he could hear the pounding of the other runners' feet. With a final spurt of speed, he flung himself across the finish line.

"The winner!" Dave yelled.

The whole cabin surrounded Mick and lifted him on their shoulders. "QUICK MICK! QUICK MICK!" they cheered.

Audi handed the banner to Varmint. "Just wait till next year," he said as he walked away.

"This will look great above *my* bunk!" Varmint called after him. "Come on, guys!" he said to his cabin. "Snacks at the Trading Post are on me today!"

Mick and Herbie were brushing their teeth. The rest of the cabin was already in bed. Herbie slid his toothbrush up his sleeve and began flossing, standing on the ledge of the mirror and staring at his shiny reflection.

"Field Day was great, huh Herbie?"

Herbie grunted through his gold floss.

"And wasn't it swell about Varmint winning this year?"

Herbie put the floss away and looked at Mick. "Come on, kid. Just because you fooled all the others doesn't mean you fooled me, too!"

"What d'you mean?"

"I mean we both know you didn't really win that race."

Mick poked at the glob of toothpaste he had dropped in the sink. "Sure I did."

"Humph!" Herbie said in disgust. "You cut through the cones on the third turn. That's how you got so far ahead—'Quick Mick!' Ha!"

Mick looked at Herbie. "Okay, so I took a shortcut. But it was for a good cause. Varmint really deserved to win. I was just helping him out."

"So you're really just a good-deed-doer, right? Wrong! You *lied* to everyone, Mick. You made them believe you had run the course when you hadn't. You let them think you were the hero of the hour. And you let your whole cabin down."

"I did not! Because of me, my whole cabin won!"

"Not really, kid. They're all just a part of your gigantic lie."

"Did anybody else see me—you know, cut across?"

Herbie nodded.

"Dave?"

"Someone even more important."

Mick was quiet for a moment. "God?"

"Uh-huh," Herbie said.

Mick turned and started toward his bunk. "I didn't mean to do anything wrong, Herbie. I just wanted Varmint to win. And I had the lead, and there was this bend. And the next thing I knew I had cut through the woods and come out way ahead. I just wanted Varmint to win . . ."

"Winning is important," Herbie said. "But honesty is, too. And nothing good ever really comes from doing something dishonest—no matter how noble or selfless you may convince yourself the act is."

"So now what?" Mick sighed as he climbed into bed. "If I tell, Varmint will lose the banner, the gang will hate me, and Dave will probably hang me by my thumbs from Mt. Wood."

"And if you don't tell?"

"The real winner will be cheated out of first place in the race. I'll be miserable. And I'll be letting God down, won't I?"

A faint glimmer in the darkness told Mick that Herbie was smiling. "You're learning, kid. And that miserable feeling you have is your conscience. The Holy Spirit is helping you learn right from wrong, giving you the courage to do the *right* instead of the *easy* thing."

"But that's your job, isn't it, Herbie?"

The smile faded. "I can't do it nearly as well as he can, kid." A long pause. "Besides, you see, there are other kids who need me, too. And—"

"You mean you won't always be my guardian angel?" Mick interrupted.

"I've been meaning to talk to you . . ."

Just then the tiny reading light over Varmint's bunk switched on.

"Guess Varmint can't sleep, either," Mick said. He sat for a minute on the side of his bunk, biting his bottom lip and looking at the banner over Varmint's bed. "Could we have that talk later, Herbie? Right now there's something I've got to do." Mick slid off his bunk and walked toward the light.

"Sure, kid," Herbie said. "Later would be just fine with me."

* * *

. . . have a clear conscience and desire to live honorably in every way.
Hebrews 13:18

Angel in My Backpack   99

Day 24

"Pull those covers tight!" Varmint said. "And be sure to sweep under the beds. We don't have a chance of winning 'Clean Cabin' unless this place is spotless!"

Spike retucked the blanket on his bed. Jeff got the broom from the corner and began sweeping under each bunk.

"How's the bathroom look, Mick?" Varmint asked on his way outside to empty the trash cans.

Mick was scrubbing the sink with an old toothbrush. "Okay, but I can't get some of these stains out."

"Make sure there's not even one chewing gum wrapper out there!" Varmint yelled to Paul and the other boys who were picking up around the outside of the cabin.

Mick finished cleaning the bathroom and shined the faucets with a soft cloth. "Somebody come hold the dustpan for me!" Jeff called, bending over a pile of dust balls and dirt.

Varmint stood in the middle of the room and surveyed the cabin. Beds were made, footlockers closed, floor clean. "Looks good to me," he said. "Let's just hope Squirt likes it."

After riflery the boys raced back to their cabin. If they won "Clean Cabin," Squirt would post the award on their door for everyone in camp to see. They bounded up the steps and stood on the porch looking at the door.

There was nothing on it.

"We lost again!" Jeff said, pounding the porch rail with his fist. "Every day we try and try. And every day we lose. What's the use?"

"Hey," Varmint said, "we'll get it one of these days. At least we have a nice, clean cabin to come back to."

"Big deal!" Paul said as they shuffled inside.

Next morning, when it came time to clean the cabin, all the boys just sat on their bunks.

"Every day we lose. What's the use?"

"Come on!" Varmint said. "Let's get this place in shape."

"Why?" Paul asked, tossing a gum wrapper to the floor. "We never win anyway."

"Yeah," Jeff said, "we're sick of cleaning and straightening and hoping."

"Let's see how Squirt likes our cabin this morning!" Mick said, turning the trash can upside down and spilling trash all over the floor.

"Yeah!" Spike yelled, mussing his covers and scattering comic books around his bunk.

"Hey, cut it out!" Varmint yelled.

But it was too late. Everyone began turning over suitcases, wadding up sleeping bags, spreading trash, and throwing wet towels all over the bathroom. Soon the cabin looked as though a tornado had passed through it.

"There." Spike smiled. "Squirt's in for a real surprise today!"

"That was really dumb, guys," Varmint said, shaking his head.

"No dumber than working every day for nothing!" Mick said as the boys ran out the cabin door.

When they came back to their cabin after lunch, the boys were surprised at how messy it really was. "Wow," Mick said, "we really did a great job of junking up this place."

"For sure," Spike said, kicking his way through piles of clothes to his bunk.

"Where's my tennis racket?" Jeff yelled, throwing trash and sleeping bags.

"Who knows!" Mick said. "I've got to find my swim trunks."

"Come on," Jeff pleaded. Help me find it. I'll be late for my lesson."

"Is this it?" Paul asked, pulling on a handle sticking out of a pile of wet towels.

"No, that's mine!" Spike said, grabbing it.

Everyone stood knee-deep in clutter, looking around the cabin.

"Well," Mick sighed. "Guess there's only one thing to do."

"You don't mean—" Paul began.

"Of course I do!" Mick said. "We've got to clean up this place, or we'll never be able to find any of our stuff."

"Right," Varmint said from the doorway. "And you'll have to miss swimming to do it. See you all later!" He grabbed his swim trunks from the clothesline behind the cabin and headed toward the pool.

It took a long time to sort through the mess and collect the trash. Finally, the cabin was clean. The boys lay on their bunks, sweaty and tired.

"Well," Herbie said, sitting on the foot of Mick's bunk, "wasn't that fun?"

"No, definitely not," Mick said.

Herbie took off his halo and began polishing it with his sleeve. "You know, kid, you can't give up just because something doesn't come easily. Look at Columbus. Look at the Wright Brothers. The harder the work, the greater the success." Herbie put his halo back in place. "It's not enough to want something; you have to work for it, too. In fact, it's the work that really makes you appreciate winning. If Squirt drew names out of a hat every day to see who got 'Clean Cabin,' then it wouldn't mean anything."

"One thing's for sure," Mick said as he stretched out on his stomach and closed his eyes. "No more messy days for us! From now on we work for 'Clean Cabin' every single day. And if we win . . ."

"When," Herbie interrupted.

"What?"

"It's *when* you win, not *if.*"

Mick opened his eyes. "You mean—"

But with a flutter of wings and a tinkle of windchimes, Herbie was gone.

* * *

Whatever you do, work at it with all your heart, as working for the Lord, not for men.

Colossians 3:23

Day 25

"Chapel is getting to be a real drag," Jeff complained as he rummaged through his suitcase for his Bible. "Day after day after day . . ."

"No kidding!" Paul agreed. "I came to camp to play baseball, not listen to sermons. I don't know why we have to go to chapel so much."

"Church is just so *boring*!" Mick said. "Back home our morning worship service is a real yawn."

"Let's go, guys," Varmint said, sticking his head in the door.

"Do we have to?" Spike asked.

"Of course! Chapel's an important part of every day," Varmint answered.

"That's your opinion," Jeff said. "We all think it's a real waste of our time."

"Is that so?" Varmint asked, looking at each boy.

"It's not that we're down on God or anything," Mick said. "It's just that, well, sitting through chapel every day gets pretty boring."

"Too bad!" Varmint said, pulling Paul to his feet. "All of you—now! No one promised you nonstop excitement here at Camp Kickapoo. And chapel is important—that's a fact."

They were the last ones to arrive and plopped down on the back row. All around them the air smelled woodsy and wet. Leaves rustled high above their heads; beyond the clearing the river gurgled past.

Mick sat on the hard chapel bench, fanning himself with the folder of songs Buckeye had passed out. First was some singing and then a skit and then Buckeye played his guitar. Mick felt his stomach growl and wondered what was for lunch. Finally, Dave stepped up by the big wooden cross. "This is the day that the Lord has made. I will rejoice and be glad in it."

Mick looked up. That was the same thing his pastor said every Sunday at the beginning of worship service.

"Every day is the Lord's," Dave continued. "But this one is especially his, because it's Sunday. Let's try to remember that in everything we do today. Let's think more about God and all his blessings. Then tonight we'll have a special Sunday evening campfire."

"Church twice in one day," Jeff groaned as the boys left chapel. "It's worse than being at home!"

That night, Mick huddled close to the fire, watching logs blaze up in shades of red and orange. It had been a busy afternoon, and Mick was glad now to sit Indian-style near the flames, watching darkness fill the forest. Together the campers sang songs while Varmint and Buckeye played their guitars. The warm sound of Squirt's harmonica seemed to hum along with the melodies.

"And now," Dave said, in a voice as soft as the firelight, "why don't some of you share what you're thankful for?"

No one spoke for a moment. Then Beaner said, "I'm thankful for sunshine."

"I'm thankful for people who care about me," Stacey said.

Other campers spoke out. One was thankful for a letter from home; another for the fact that he hadn't been hurt when his horse accidentally stepped on his foot. "I'm thankful for new friends." Mick recognized the voice as K.C.'s.

Mick was surprised at how soon the service was over. Buckeye kept strumming his guitar as campers began filing back to their cabins. The Bucks went first. While he waited his turn to leave, Mick sat poking at the fire with a long stick. He scraped an ember from the coals and watched it cool and finally die. He pulled out another and soon its red glow cooled to a lifeless black.

"Warriors may go now," Buckeye said at last.

The boys stayed close together on the trail. The darkness seemed to tug at their heels. "That was pretty cool, as church services go," said Jeff.

"Yeah," Paul admitted. "It wasn't too bad, except for the mosquitoes."

Back in the cabin, the boys took quick showers and went straight to bed. Mick finished brushing his teeth and tiptoed to his bunk.

"How'd you like the service?" Herbie asked.

"It was sure better than real church, where I have to dress up and sit on pews. You know, Herbie, lots of times I feel like Jeff. Church is a real drag!"

Herbie hovered over Mick's bed, a soft glow in the darkness. "Church isn't going to be a thrill a minute, kid. Few things in life are. And sometimes you may think church is boring or a waste of time. But it never is—because the church is really the body of Christ, the family of God here on earth. It's important for Christians to meet together and encourage each other, to gain strength from worshiping together."

"But can't you be a Christian without going to church all the time? I could read my Bible before I went skateboarding on Sunday afternoon or pray while I was baiting my hook down at the lake."

Herbie sat down on the pillow next to Mick. "Remember those embers you scraped from the fire tonight?" Mick nodded. "What happened to them?" Herbie asked.

"They stopped burning and then died out."

"It's the same with Christians, kid. Together they are a source of warmth and light. They gather strength and enthusiasm and courage from one another. But when left alone, it's easy for them to lose that light, to become discouraged. And even to die spiritually."

"You make it sound like a matter of life and death, Herbie."

"Actually, it is—spiritual life as part of Christ's church or spiritual death as a chump who tries to make it on his own."

Mick closed his eyes and snuggled into his sleeping bag. "So I can either be an ember or an ash, huh Herbie?"

"That's pretty much it, kid," Herbie said, curling up for the night in the top of Mick's backpack and covering himself with his wings. "An ember or an ash."

* * *

Let us not give up meeting together, as some are in the habit of doing, but let us encourage one another.

Hebrews 10:25

Day 26

"Good try!" Beaner said as she undid Paul's harness. "You'll get it next time for sure!"

Mick looked at Paul's face. His cheeks were red and his hands fumbled with the helmet. Mick knew exactly how he felt. Mad. Embarrassed. Like a loser.

"So, are you next?" Herbie asked.

Mick shook his head. "Naw, I'd just make a fool of myself. Again." He looked up at Mt. Wood. It seemed to have grown taller, its hand- and footholds stretched further apart. Just thinking about climbing it made Mick's chest ache, the way it did when he'd been underwater too long.

"Come on, kid. That first time was just for practice. Try it again!"

"No way, Herbie."

"Why not?"

"Because," Mick poked at his shoestrings with a stick, "because if I don't try, I can't fail."

"True, but you can't *win* either."

"Who's next?" Beaner asked. "We have time for one more climb."

"Do it!" Herbie urged, poking Mick in the back.

"Okay, okay." Mick stood up.

"All right!" Flounder called down from the tower. "You can do it, Mick! Just don't give up this time!"

Wearing the helmet and harness, Mick took a deep

breath and reached for his first handhold. He pushed up
with his legs, moving first one foot, then the other. His
calves felt full of knots. Already his hands were shaking.

"Move one contact point at a time," Beaner said. "The
next foothold is up and to your left."

Mick fumbled to find the block of wood. His feet
slipped, and for a second he hung by his fingertips. Then
he felt the short firmness under his toe. He pressed his
cheek against the warm side of Mt. Wood. "Slow down,"
he said, gulping for air. His heartbeat sounded in his ears
like the inside of seashells. Sweat soaked his fingers.

Every muscle in his arms and legs felt ready to snap.
"I can't," he told himself.

He glanced down at Beaner and felt his stomach
lurch.

"Come on, Mick! You're almost there!" Mick squinted
up into the sun; Flounder's face was bending toward him.

Mick tried to push, but his legs had turned to Jell-O.
He was going to fail again! For an instant, he felt like
throwing up. His hands were slipping. Mick closed his eyes
and thought about falling.

"Come on, Mick! Don't give up now!"

"One more push!"

The voices of his friends floated up, thin and echoey.

Angel in My Backpack

"Once more," Mick grunted, licking sweat from his lips. He opened his eyes and thought how good it would feel to stand on top of Mt. Wood.

And then he pushed.

Mick hung over the railing while Flounder patted his back and dragged him onto the landing. "You did it, Mick! You climbed Mt. Wood!"

Mick lay on his back feeling the pain in his legs, the numbness in his fingertips. Each breath was like a knife-stab. He opened his eyes. The sky seemed close enough to touch!

From below came clapping and whistling and shouts of "Yea, Mick!" Mick slipped off his helmet so he could hear them better. His hands were still shaking and his knees a bit weak as he stood, smiling, and waved from the top of Mt. Wood. His smile got even bigger when he saw that K.C. was part of the cheering crowd.

"Congratulations!" Herbie said, sitting on the railing.

"I did it, Herbie!" Mick laughed. "I'm not a loser—I'm a winner!" Then he climbed down the back ladder and was soon surrounded by campers offering their congratulations.

"I knew it all along, kid." Herbie smiled as Mick and K.C. walked toward the drinking fountain.

* * *

Let us not become weary in doing good, for at the proper time we will reap a harvest if we do not give up.
Galatians 6:9

Day 27

T his reminds me of a mud hike," Spike said, burying his thumb in the wet clay.

The boys sat at long tables outside the craft hut. "All right," Squirt began, "you are about to turn this lump of clay into a work of art. Just think of the clay as an extension of yourself. Pick it up and hold it in your hand."

Mick picked up his clay and began working it. Soon it felt soft and stretchy, like just-chewed bubble gum.

"And now—create!" Squirt said.

Mick stared at his clay. Create? He looked around. Spike was rolling out a worm. Jeff was making a soccer ball complete with designs. Paul was just looking at his clay, too. Finally, Mick broke the clay into three pieces and, rolling each one into a ball, made a mud-colored snowman.

"Very good!" Squirt almost sang as she looked at each one. "Now tomorrow we'll begin in earnest on our projects!"

The next day, Mick rolled his snowman into one huge lump, then worked with the clay until it was warm and pliable. Squirt showed them pictures of pots and vases made by ancient Indian tribes.

"And now, boys," she smiled, "choose any pot design, or create your own. When you've finished molding, we'll paint and fire them in the kiln. And then you'll have your very own work of art!"

112   *Day 27*

Angel in My Backpack

Mick looked again at his lump of clay. It didn't look like it had much chance of becoming anything, much less a work of art.

Every day, during craft time, Mick worked on his pot. He decided to make his round at the bottom and then narrower at the top with a broad lip around the opening— like a vase for flowers. Instead it kept looking like a pop bottle someone had stepped on. So he kept squashing the clay back into a lump so he could begin again. And again.

On his fifth day of working on the pot, most of the other boys were painting bright Indian designs on their creations. Mick looked at his latest effort. "Ug-ly!" he said, flattening it pancake-thin. Then he got up and started down the path toward his cabin, kicking at pebbles along the way.

"What's this, a temper tantrum?" Herbie asked. "I hear you artistic people can be awfully moody."

"Maybe I'm moody, but I'm sure not artistic! Face it, Herbie. I can't do anything right!"

"What you need, kid, is more self-confidence. And lots of patience—with your clay and with yourself."

"What I really need is some talent. And a few more muscles couldn't hurt either. Or how about a brain transplant so I'll be smart enough to wash my clothes without burying the laundry hut in soapsuds." Mick sat down at the edge of the parking lot. He pulled at a weed growing up through the gravel. "I can't face that stupid clay any more, Herbie!"

Herbie fluttered in front of Mick. "Don't expect your pot to be perfect, kid. Even professional potters are always having to start over. Only God gets things right the first time. Just like when he formed Adam out of the dust of the earth, molding and shaping man into his own image. Then he breathed into him the breath of life. So—God's the original potter. And he's still busy molding."

"Molding what?"

"Well, you for instance. God is shaping your life

through the things that happen to you, through the people and places you experience, through the friends you make. He is molding you every time you read your Bible or talk to him in prayer."

"God must be pretty disappointed with what a mess I am," Mick said.

"Not at all! You're growing and learning every day. But then, God is not only talented, he's also patient when it comes to his creations. And he never gives up on one."

Mick stood up and threw the plucked weed into the grass. "One more time, Herbie. I'll try to make that stupid clay pot just one more time!"

Mick settled himself back on the bench and took up his clay. Herbie helped smooth out the wrinkles on the sides as Mick formed the base. After a while, Mick looked at the piece. "What d'you think so far, Herbie?"

Herbie flew around and looked at it from all angles. "I think if you keep on like this, you'll be surprised how well this vase turns out!"

And several days later, when Mick took his vase out of the kiln, he had to admit Herbie was right.

* * *

O Lord, you are our Father. We are the clay, you are the potter; we are all the work of your hand.

Isaiah 64:8

Day 28

K.C. stood in front of the open pop machine, waiting to pass out the cold cans. Afternoon activities were almost over, and everyone was getting anxious for "pop stop." Suddenly, the sounds of "The 1812 Overture" blared from the loudspeakers situated high above the playing fields. And dozens of thirsty campers ran toward the Trading Post for their daily soda. As they lined up according to cabins, counselors passed out old bottle caps to those who had asked to have pop put on their Trading Post account.

While another Ranger collected the bottle caps, K.C. handed out the soft drinks. "What'll it be?" she asked repeatedly. "Root beer, orange, cola, or punch?"

Mick's cabin was near the back of the line. They stood fingering the prickly edges of the bottle caps and feeling the sweat creep down their backs.

"I could drink a whole liter of pop," Mick said. "Without even coming up for air."

"Me, too," Paul said. "I hate only getting one lousy can a day. It's our money; we ought to be able to spend as much as we want on whatever we want."

"Yeah," Jeff said. "Then they give us these crummy bent-up bottle caps to use instead."

At last it was their turn. One by one the boys in Mick's cabin stepped up and ordered what they wanted to drink.

"I'll have a root beer," Mick said when K.C. turned around.

"One root beer," she said, reaching in the back for one that was extra cold.

When Mick joined the others, they were talking about money again. I'd buy an oil well in Texas. That'd keep on making me money for a long time," Spike said.

"I'd buy lots and lots of cars. A different color for every day of the week. Maybe even the month!" Jeff laughed.

"A gourmet restaurant," Flounder said. "One that serves seafood and rich desserts."

Mick took long drinks of his root beer, feeling its coolness ripple down into his stomach. "How about you, Mick?" Spike asked. "If you had tons of money, what would you buy?"

Mick smiled. "That's easy," he said. "Disneyland!"

That evening, Herbie and Mick sat outside watching the stars come out. "They look like diamonds scattered on black velvet," Mick said.

"If they really were diamonds," Herbie replied, "some human would raise an expedition and drag them back to sell."

Mick laughed. "You're probably right. I guess no one ever thinks he has enough money. Why is that, Herbie?"

"Greed! Pure and simple! Unlike other animals who take only what they need, man likes to horde, to have more than his fellow creatures. He wants the sense of power money can bring." Herbie fluffed his wings in disgust. "Money makes men foolish and self-centered."

"But what about all the good things people do with money? Things like giving to orphanages and to cancer research and to help hungry people around the world. Isn't money good then?"

"No one ever thinks he has enough money. Why is that, Herbie?"

Herbie sighed. "Of course money can be used for good, kid. It's just that it so seldom is. Money is not what causes so much trouble. It's the *love* of money that leads to sin and evil. Money has a certain power of its own, convincing its owner of his need for more. And more. Until worldly goods and gold become more important than family or friends—or even God.

"Jesus spoke often about that problem when he was here on earth twenty centuries ago; it's nothing new. But it's something you have to watch out for, kid. Because it sneaks up on you. First you want one thing, then another. Soon you need a part-time job to keep up with all your wants. And soon after that there's no time for church or Bible reading. And you begin to think how great you are because of the clothes you wear or the car you drive or the people you run around with. And somewhere in the shuffle to get more money, God is left behind. It happens all the time."

"I'd never thought about money *causing* problems," Mick said quietly. "It always seemed like the *answer* to problems."

"I know," Herbie said. "That's what makes it so dangerous."

The moon had come out now. Its silver whiteness surrounded Mick and Herbie. "If the stars were really diamonds," Mick said, "then the moon would be a giant pearl." He was quiet for a moment. "But I'm glad they're not. This way their beauty belongs to everyone."

"You wouldn't want to own the moon and stars?"

"No way!"

"How about Disneyland?" Herbie asked.

"Well," Mick grinned, "only a little tiny part of it."

"The roller coaster, right?" Herbie guessed.

Mick shook his head.

"How about the log ride where you always get wet?"

"Nope."

"Then it must be the bumper cars."

"Wrong."

"Then what?" Herbie asked. "What one little part would you want to own?"

"The ticket booth!" Mick laughed. "That way I could ride the rides any time I wanted!"

* * *

"Do not store up for yourselves treasures on earth . . . But store up for yourselves treasures in heaven. . . . You cannot serve both God and Money."

Matthew 6:19–20, 24

Day 29

T he rain came in thick sheets—soaking everything, filling the paths with wide, muddy puddles.

"It's just got to stop!" Spike said as they looked out from the porch. "This could ruin our whole closing campfire! And closing campfire is the best thing about Camp Kickapoo!"

"No, it isn't," Paul said. "It's the saddest. Everybody cries and hugs and sings those sad songs about friendship."

"Okay, so it's sad," Spike said, catching a raindrop. "But it's also neat—with the Indian and everything. Stop, rain! Do you hear me!"

The rain finally settled into a foggy drizzle. "Think we'll still have campfire?" Mick asked.

Spike shrugged his shoulders. "Who knows?"

Varmint came running across the field and up the steps. "Campfire's on, guys! Dave's putting dry firewood out now. Load up on bug spray and let's go!"

The boys cheered and got ready to leave. "Tonight's when Sagamores are chosen, too," Spike told Mick as he sprayed Mick's back with insect repellent. Mick looked at the single bead around Spike's neck and remembered what K.C. had said about how only a few campers get to be Sagamores.

120   *Day 29*

The fire was roaring when the boys got there. Buckeye led the group in a few funny songs. Suddenly, an Indian chief dressed in fringed leather vest and pants rode bareback out of the forest. He slid off his horse and walked toward the fire, his moccasins making no noise on the wet grass. His huge headdress was filled with white feathers tipped in red and black.

"It is time!" the chief said, his voice booming across the dusk. "Some have been chosen Sagamore. Even now a runner approaches."

Mick looked in the direction he pointed. An Indian brave came running toward them, carrying a flaming torch in one hand and a rolled piece of parchment in the other. He gave the parchment to the chief and held the torch near so he could read its words.

"To be chosen Sagamore is a great honor," the Indian chief said. "Let me read to you the creed of the Sagamore Council, for all true Sagamore must live accordingly. 'As a Sagamore I will be worthy of trust. I will love the world around me, and each day will bring new adventures. I will do what needs to be done without being asked. I am happy with life and with myself, yet I will always try harder to be the best I can be. All this because God, the Great Spirit, is most important to me; the other fellow is second only to him; and I am third. I am a Sagamore.'"

Angel in My Backpack

The silence was deep and serious. Mick could hear the crackling of the fire and the call of an owl deep in the pine forest. "And now the names of the new Sagamores," the chief said. "If you are chosen, come forward with pride and humility." Blue flames licked around the torch as the chief read the names. One by one the chosen campers came forward. Mick recognized Stacey and Critter. When nine campers stood with the chief he said, "And the last to become Sagamore is Mick."

"Congratulations!" Spike whispered, patting Mick on the back and pushing him to his feet. Mick stood with the others, feeling the warmth of the campfire on his cheeks. Sagamore! He had never even dreamed . . .

"Sagamores will now join hands for your pilgrimage to the sacred council ring. There shall be no words," the chief commanded, "for none are needed. My brave shall show you the way."

Mick gripped the hands of those closest to him. Together they started into the forest, and Mick soon found himself wrapped in silence and darkness. The path grew narrower, and the Sagamores bumped into wet leaves and bushes that crowded their way.

Finally they came to a clearing. Beaner stood beside a huge cross made of logs lashed together with leather straps. The brave touched his torch to a pile of wood at its base, and a campfire burst to life.

Beaner smiled. "Congratulations. You have earned the highest honor of Camp Kickapoo. You are a Sagamore. Please be seated."

Mick and the others sat on fallen logs near the fire. Beaner read again the 'Creed of the Sagamore Council,' talking about what each part meant. Then they all stood, and one by one they were given their Sagamore bead and a copy of the Creed. Beaner called each one of them by a special Indian name that had been chosen for him. Quiet Fawn, Little White Bear, Seeking Squirrel. When Beaner came to Mick she put the bead around his neck and said, "Go in peace, Wise Owl."

Together the Sagamores walked back to camp. Where the campfire had been was now embers. The group said quiet good-nights and started back toward their own cabins. Mick walked alone, filled with a sense of surprise and new responsibility. He touched his bead.

"Nice going, kid." Herbie glimmered like a pocket of moonlight.

"Sagamore, Herbie! Who'd have thought it?"

"I'm not surprised. What do you think of your Indian name?"

"Wise Owl? I don't know. I don't feel very wise."

"But you've learned a lot here at Camp Kickapoo— and not just archery and tennis and how to climb Mt. Wood. You've learned about yourself and other people and God."

"You're right," Mick said. "And I've learned the order those three go in, too."

Herbie smiled, as together he and Mick said the final lines from the Sagamore Creed:

"'God is most important to me, the other fellow is second only to Him, and I Am Third.'"

* * *

The fear of the Lord is the beginning of wisdom.

Psalm 111:10

Day 30

T he parking lot was filled with cars, their trunks open and waiting to be loaded with sleeping bags and backpacks and pillowcases filled with dirty laundry.

"So what do you think of Camp Kickapoo now, kid?" Herbie asked. "Let's see," he said, as the tiny gold spiral notebook fell out of his sleeve and into his hand. "As I remember it, you were worried about . . . ah, yes. Here it is: 'bean sprouts, cabin mates who'd hate you, and someone named King Kong.'"

Mick laughed. "Guess I was wrong about those things. Camp Kickapoo's great. I kind of hate to leave. Spike and Flounder and Varmint—I'm not very good at saying good-bye."

Herbie fingered the edges of his spiral. "I . . . uh . . . I know what you mean, kid."

"Hey, Mick!" Preston was waving at him, standing near his folks. "Mom, Dad—this is Mick," Preston beamed. "I told you about him in my letters. He can climb Mt. Wood and play tetherball and do everything real good. And he even made Sagamore!" Preston pushed his glasses up on his nose and smiled. "We're friends."

"Nice to meet you," Mick said to the man and woman who shook his hand. "Take it easy, Preston." Mick punched him on the arm. "See you next year."

124   *Day 30*

Angel in My Backpack

Mick went on into the Trading Post. He smiled when he saw the T-shirt hanging on the wall.

"Hi there, Mick," Dave said. "All packed for home?"

Mick nodded. "But first I want to buy one of those." He pointed at the T-shirt. On it was a picture of a man climbing a mountain, and behind him glowed a huge, orange sun. In big letters it said: "I Climbed Mt. Wood."

Dave laughed. "You sure earned it!" Mick waved as he turned and walked back outside to the parking lot. He took off his old T-shirt and put on his new one.

Spike was loading his stuff onto the bus. "So long, Mick," he said. "Let's keep in touch. We Sagamores have to stick together!" Mick held out his hand so they could shake. "I'm afraid that's not good enough," Spike said, hugging Mick. "Bye, friend."

One by one the cars headed up the hill and out to the highway. It looked like a parade of suntanned, smiling kids.

Mick spotted K.C. walking toward a pickup truck, loaded down with suitcase and pillow and sleeping bag. He ran to help her.

"Thanks," she said as he took the suitcase. "It always seems heavier going home."

"Mine's heavier because all the clothes in it are so dirty!" Mick laughed.

"Nice shirt," K.C. said, smiling.

They walked in silence. The air smelled of pine, and the sun was warm on their backs. Mick slid the suitcase into the back of the truck and helped K.C. with the rest of her things. He kicked at the clump of grass growing in the driveway. "Uh—camp's been great, hasn't it?" he said.

"Uh-huh," K.C. said.

"I mean—the food and canoeing and chapel and mud hikes." Mick paused. "And new friends."

K.C. smiled. "Especially new friends." Mick looked up. He could feel his cheeks redden. "I have to go now," she said. "My dad's waiting."

"Okay, sure. Have a good trip home. See you next year." They stood looking at each other for a moment.

"Bye," K.C. said as she gave Mick a quick, awkward hug.

Mick started back to his cabin to get his stuff, smiling about all the things he and Herbie could remember together.

Suddenly he stopped. Where was Herbie, anyway? The sound of windchimes tinkled on the air. Mick whirled around to see K.C.'s truck pulling out of the drive, something shiny glinting on its back bumper. Mick felt his knees go weak when he realized what it was. A gold smile. Herbie's gold smile!

"Herbie, come back!" he yelled. "I need you!" The weight of his Sagamore bead lay strangely heavy on Mick's neck.

"Others second," he heard a familiar voice say.

"And I am third," Mick said, touching the bead.

K.C. leaned out the window and waved. Mick waved back. "Good-bye, Herbie," he whispered. "And thanks."

K.C. disappeared back inside the truck, but Mick kept waving—at the bouncing halo and bright smile of Herbie, hanging onto K.C.'s bumper. Till at last pickup truck and guardian angel vanished over the hill.

* * *

"So do not fear, for I am with you; do not be dismayed, for I am your God. I will strengthen you and help you."
Isaiah 41:10

Angel in My Backpack